NOMAD

First Novel of the Nomad Series

Lawrence Henry

Table of Contents

To those who fight for themselves and others in the darkest of times, and to those who stand by them with unwavering strength and love. This book is dedicated to the resilient and courageous souls who refuse to give up, even when faced with seemingly insurmountable challenges.

Acknowledgements

My late father, Lloyd Henry Jr. – We didn't always see eye-to-eye on fiction and its uses to society, but without his lessons on critical thinking and logic, this would have been a very different book.

My mother, Patricia Haby-Henry – A constant source of love and support at the most difficult times.

My brothers: Lloyd R. Henry Sr., & James M. Henry – Co-conspirators in creativity and faith, with a penchant for goofy humor.

My sisters: Tina Brock, Hagan N. Whiteside, & Pamela R. Henry – Fonts of support, love, and inspiration.

My wife: Amanda Dishroom – For all the reminders to be kind to myself, at the times I wanted to let go of my passion.

My children: Liana E. Henry, & Mathias D. Henry – Without these two knuckleheads, I would have probably finished this years ago, but it would have suffered for it.

My editors: Wes Imrisek, A.R.Grimes, & Huckleberry Rahr – These three didn't just help me edit this novel. They're a major part of why I felt motivated to finish it. They're wonderful friends, and incredible authors. I am forever grateful for their near constant contributions (also, for putting up with me when I'd overthink some scene or other and start panicking) to the project.

If any of you happen to read this book, thank you for tolerating me.

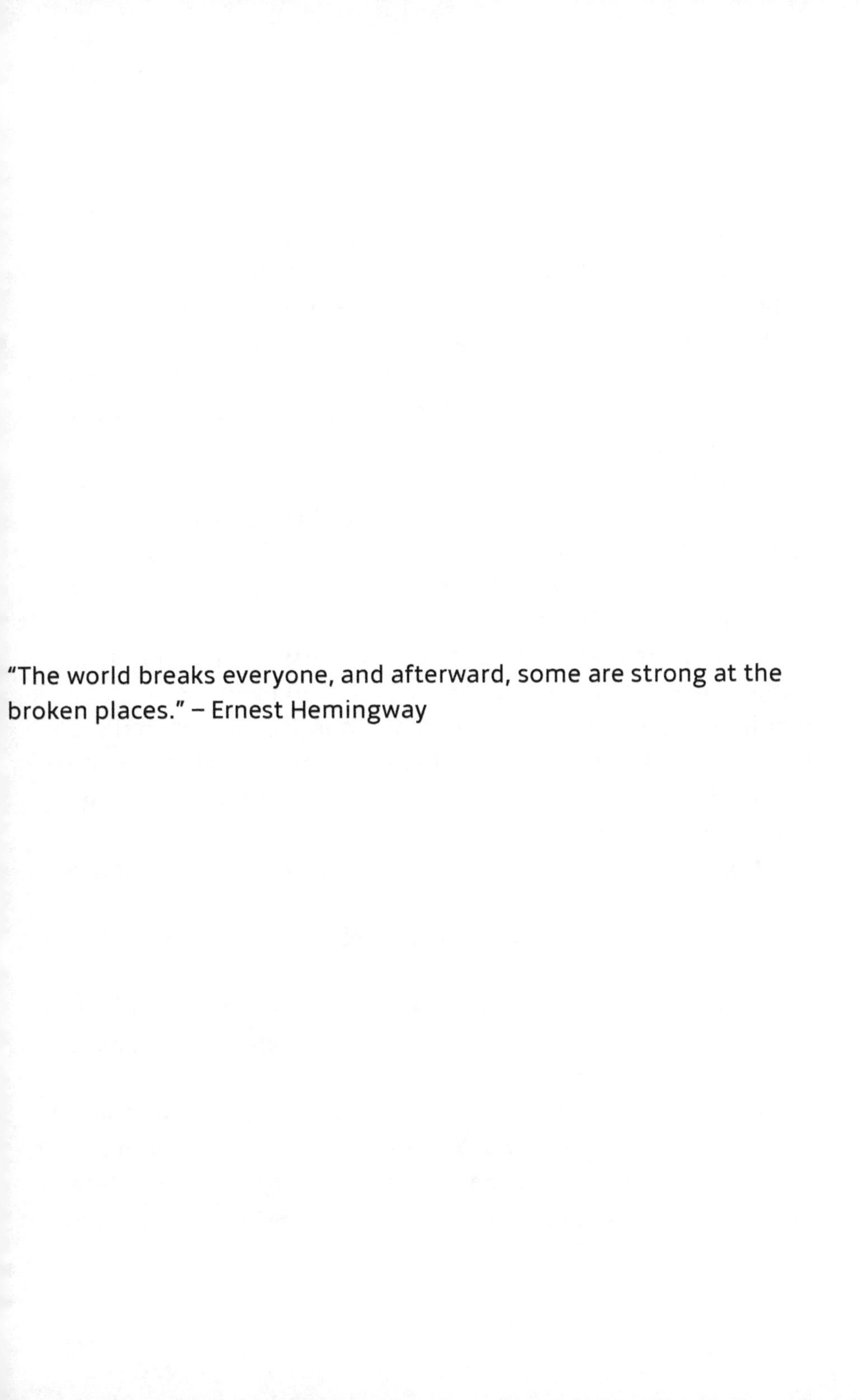

"The world breaks everyone, and afterward, some are strong at the broken places." – Ernest Hemingway

1 The Scars Above

Gauze bandages squeezed Steven's stinging knuckles. A reminder of the slick coating of blood from the fight an hour earlier. His heart pounded again at the memory.

He smothered a creeping smile at the memory of fear in Curtis's face: hazel eyes wide and glistening; his lips trembling and bloodied. Steeling himself for the lecture ahead, Steven locked eyes with the principal.

Principal Hogan had stuffed his office to the brim with inspirational posters, calendars, and pillows. It even had a painting of a sunflower on one wall, across from the pale particle-board desk. Across the room sat a squat couch with lemon-colored pillows.

Behind the main desk sat another desk with a computer, flanked by equally drab shelves covered in even more happiness vomit. A few pictures of what Steven decided were the principal's family, and an 'I teach, what's your superpower?' plaque. Even with all the accouterments, a cold, uninviting atmosphere permeated the room.

Hogan said, "I'd like to say you've learned your lesson, son. But I know better."

Steven looked up sharply with eyes narrowed. "You do know better."

Hogan put his hands up. Then, he rubbed at his chin, "That was a poor choice of words, I'll admit. But what do you expect? You hurt Curtis quite badly."

Steven rubbed his face. "Let me put it this way. A student tells you he's being bullied. You say there's nothing you can do about it. Tell him to ignore the bully. The situation escalates due to violent provocation from the bully. What you don't seem to see is that I tried it your way. Stop pretending you're disappointed in me when you're the one who failed. I don't expect anything from you, which is exactly what I got."

"That still doesn't give you the right to take matters into your own hands."

Steven grunted and shifted in the plush seat. If he could get away with just standing up and walking out, he would. They were talking in circles now.

"If you boys didn't live in the same house, I'd send you home right now. Instead, I'm putting you on in-school suspension until I can get in touch with the director of y'all's home for a more adequate solution."

Steven shrugged.

"You boys have so much potential. Are you trying to throw away your future?"

Steven chuckled. "What future?"

Adults always thought about the future. They kept talking like he had one. He already had a past he couldn't stand and a present that wasn't much better. Steven wasn't sure why, but he just felt driven toward survival by whatever means he could conjure. In his mind, there were only two real ways to stop violence coming at him. He could either allow it to harm him, and live with whatever consequences the enemy had planned, or he could respond with greater, more efficient force.

"Steven," Principal Hogan breathed out a pained sigh, "You've been through quite a lot for someone so young. I recognize that the situation with you and Curtis is troublesome because of your proximity. But you do have a future. And it can be a bright one, if you utilize your potential."

Steven was tired of the 'potential' speech. He cleared his throat, stopping Hogan before he got too far into it.

"Speaking of potential, I'm late for class. Can I go now?"

Hogan sighed. "Just...think about what I said, Steven. All I want is to see you succeed."

I bet you say that to all the troubled teens.

Steven stood, scooping up his backpack from the floor. He accepted the offered pink disciplinary slip and turned to the door. He left the door open, to allow Hogan's concerned gaze to follow him through the main office of Blue Rock High School and nodded to the young brown-haired woman behind the desk, although he couldn't remember her name. Hearing footsteps, Steven looked back to see Principal Hogan walk over and slowly shut his office door.

The young woman glanced from the door to Steven and back. The nameplate on her desk read Ladeen.

Ladeen said, "I take it that didn't go so well?"

Steven grinned. "Not for him."

"I heard you and Curtis got into a fight. What happened?"

Word traveled fast, apparently. Granted, it had only been long enough for the lunch hour to be over for a few minutes.

"Hit me with his lunch tray."

"Considering the results, I don't think he'll be trying that again."

Steven chuckled, "Never know with idiots like him."

"True," she said with a knowing smile. "You'd think I'd know, huh?"

The comment caught him. It felt too specific. Then, it dawned on him.

Steven grimaced. "You two are...I'm sorry to be so callous about it."

Ladeen laughed, "You're good. Curtis is a good guy, but he can be a little dense. To hear him talk, though, he was rather mean about you."

"Well, you know him better than I do."

The knowing smile returned. "You could say that."

Steven turned at the sound of Hogan's office door opening again.

Hogan said, "Don't you have to be in class, Steven?"

Steven left the office, backpack on one shoulder, staring at the tiled floor as he walked the halls, weaving through the crowd of shouting students. He entered art class just as the fifth-period late bell rang. In the classroom, the smell of markers was overlaid with the acrid, pungent scent of cheap coffee. Several long tables were spaced oddly around the room, many of them pushed back-to-back.

One girl, dressed in a decidedly theatrical Victorian manner—puffy sleeves and all—chattered on with another whose makeup couldn't possibly get any darker. The two sketched as they talked, eyeshadow occasionally rolling her eyes at the antics around her.

A couple of the guys from the football team tossed wads of paper at one another from opposite corners of the room. Mr. Sorensen had done all he could to stop them from being a disruption, but it wasn't enough. Steven dropped into a seat and pulled a sketchbook and pencil from his bag as Mr. Sorensen droned on about something in an airy southern drawl.

Principal Hogan...well, he continued to be his usual annoyingly helpful self. There was a weird energy in the air that no one else seemed to notice. The prissy blonde absently flirting with one of the football guys popped gum and filed her nails incessantly. The football guy leaned over and pulled her face into his.

They made a wet sound as he looked like he was trying to swallow her mouth. *Like an overgrown fish.* She shoved him away, laughing and swatting. Steven swallowed bile and shook his head, pulling his sketchbook close to doodle away the time.

Someone cleared their throat. Steven looked up from an absent-minded doodle to see Grace staring at him. Other students in the room were paired up, taking the opportunity to talk and laugh when they should have been doing something *artistic.*

"You didn't hear me, did you?" asked Grace, playing with her soft blonde hair.

Steven shrugged. "Nope. A lot on my mind, I guess."

She narrowed her eyes and fought to hide a mischievous smile that kept seeming to creep back in. "Fighting will do that, I'm sure."

He raised an eyebrow. "Well, somebody's gotten bold."

Grace huffed, "What's that supposed to mean?"

"You've made a bold assumption." He lifted a hand. "This isn't on my mind at all. That fight's over and done with."

She sighed. "Would you like to partner up with me today? We're supposed to be sketching one another in pairs."

Steven made a show of looking around at the other pairs. A paper ball hit him in the forehead. The guy that threw it cackled, hands up. "My bad, G."

Steven rolled his eyes. "Lucky me, I'm last pick."

"Don't even, Steven." She giggled at herself. "I've been trying to get your attention since you walked in the door. It's not my fault you don't pay attention to anything."

Steven shrugged.

"Okay, Grace. You got me. Now what?"

"Now, draw..." she said, pointing a finger gun. She gave a sly smile and rolled her eyes.

Steven cracked a smile and flipped to a new page in his sketchbook. He took in the girl in front of him. Green eyes the color of a field in spring met his gaze as she smiled, a nervous twitch to her lips, thin and pink. Her golden hair was pinned with a series of decorative, sparkling purple clips. She wore a form-fitting violet t-shirt. A pair of skinny jeans and slightly scuffed white sneakers finished her look. Steven adjusted his grip on the pencil and started sketching lightly on the pad.

"Tell me, then," he said, "why you're so intent on getting my attention."

Her face scrunched. "To be honest, I'm not sure."

"Huh..." He set his gaze on her. "Let me guess, you want to fix me from being a brooding mess?"

"It's not like that at all. You like to walk around like you don't care about anything. Like you're completely cold-hearted. But I think there's more to you than that."

"I see. And that crazy girl you hang with? Mirena? What's the deal with her always flirting with me?"

Grace laughed. "Mirena's more than just a friend. She's my cousin on my dad's side. She calls herself a 'love guru'. That's been her way of trying to push me into admitting my crush on you."

He glanced up at the last statement, noting how red Grace's face had become.

"I guess it worked?" Steven paused for a moment while he stared at her pointed nose. "If it helps, I've known you had a crush on me for a year. Unfortunately, my headphones only cancel out so much. On the other hand, if you're waiting for me to ask you out, I'm sorry to disappoint you. I may be just as cold-hearted as I seem."

Grace shook her head. "The proof is right there in your eyes. You don't seriously believe what you just told me, and you're a terrible liar. And, for the record, I'm done waiting for you to do anything, slowpoke. Will you take me to the dance?"

Steven blinked, his hand stopping in the middle of a pencil stroke. He laid the drawing pad face-down so she couldn't see it, set the pencil on top, and stared at her, incredulous. Before he knew what was happening, she snatched the pad and looked at it, breaking into a wide smile.

"This looks nothing like me, but she's pretty for a stick figure. Nice boobs, too. My turn."

Grace appeared to ignore the widening of Steven's eyes, and the blush that crossed his cheeks. She returned the pad with a smile, turned to a new page in her own sketch pad and began to mimic his serious face as she scratched her pencil across the page. The emotions and light that played across her face brought a soft smile to Steven's lips.

Steven chuckled. "Sorry, I'm not that good at drawing."

"That's okay. I'm not much better. Maybe you just haven't found your art form?"

He haltingly glanced at her. "I don't know. Maybe."

"You know, maybe we should have taken auto shop instead."

They used the rest of the class time talking about their home lives. Steven, of course, leaving out the classified bits of living in a dorm on the Arsenal. Grace, for her part, talked about living with her cousin.

"Sounds like she can be a bit of a pain, huh?"

Grace laughed a little too hard, slipping out of her chair and landing on the tile floor. She quieted, covering her face with her hands, eyes wide. Eyeshadow looked concerned, but Grace put up a thumb, revealing a reddened, smiling face.

"Go big or go home, I guess," said one of the jocks, laughing.

"Yeah," shouted the other. "Polish that chair yourself, or did freakazoid help?"

Steven's eyes narrowed, holding on the jock's square, joy-filled face.

The guy noticed and laughed harder. "Any time, freak show."

He focused back on as Grace grasped his hand. He grinned as he helped her back to her feet.

"Oh, you have no idea. I swear, she's so messy," said Grace, stammering to continue as though nothing had happened. "But she's pretty, and good with a guitar. I can give her credit for that. And, for not being a total klutz."

The bell rang, and they went their separate ways to their final classes for the day. Steven couldn't get his mind off the conversation he'd had with Grace. It didn't even register that he'd driven back to the base. Only when he was back in his room did it dawn on him that he'd left the school.

He sighed as he closed his door. What did she know about him? Nothing, of course. He peeled the shirt from his body and tossed it onto the hard plastic chair provided for him. It was a small room with little to distinguish it from any of the others in the building. A bed, desk with chair, small dresser, a closet, and a bathroom. He didn't believe in decorating. He wouldn't be here long enough for it to matter, anyway.

How could he explain to Grace what had brought him to Blue Rock all those years ago? He moved into the bathroom and stared at the jagged line that stretched from his right shoulder to a spot just under his ribs. The surgeon had said he'd gotten lucky.

He touched the scar where it crossed over his heart and peered into his own eyes. They were his father's eyes. A brown so dark, you could be forgiven for thinking they were black. A lack of sleep evidenced by dark circles and an almost sunken look. What the hell did Grace see in those eyes that he didn't? All he could see was the darkness.

"What am I doing, Dad?" asked Steven, feeling numb as he stared at his own face. He remembered what it looked like when those dark eyes lost the light behind them while blood pooled around the body. He shook his head, trying to clear it. It didn't work. Every time he looked at those eyes, and that scar, it reminded him. He was fighting the world alone. There were no heroes, no one to come to the rescue.

He splashed water over his face in the little sink and went back to his chair. He pulled a small bundle from a hidden compartment in his backpack and unwrapped it, revealing a gleaming pistol inside. He laid it out on the desk and stripped the parts, opening a drawer to the side and retrieving the cleaning kit.

A knock on his door drew his attention. He opened it, not at all surprised to see Captain Devyn Abaroa, an older man with a constantly sour expression.

"Steven," said Devyn, "I came to congratulate you on getting the negative attention you seem so bound and determined to receive."

"He keeps hitting me in public. This time, I hit back. Why does no one get that?"

"Sometimes you need to show restraint."

Steven's eyes widened. "Did I somehow miss the point of our training?"

"I think maybe you have. That's why you're training with the Nomad team tonight."

"Really?" said Steven, raising an eyebrow. "How's that supposed to teach me restraint?"

Devyn said, "You're reporting your insubordinate ass to the gym in three minutes or less to find out. You have your orders. Now move."

Steven sighed, reassembling the pistol and carefully packing it back into its hidden space in his bag.

"Twenty-three seconds," said Devyn, nodding, a hand on his watch. "Impressive enough, but if you're trying to break any records, you've got work to do."

Devyn tilted his head suddenly. "You haven't..."

"Would you rather I need it and not have it?" said Steven.

"I would rather," said Devyn, an intense look on his face, "you stop drawing all this attention to yourself before someone at that school decides to search your bag. They will lock you up for that. After they expel you. And who knows what Blackwood would do to you."

Steven smiled as he slid the backpack in the closet, put his boots and shirt back on and followed Devyn through austere hallways lined with numbered doors until they got to one with a special card scanner. Devyn produced a card and pressed it to the reader. The light on the device's panel turned from red to green, and the door clicked.

The hallways in this area were white with red borders. The Nomads lived in this portion of the compound, just a few doors away from the most secure locations in the facility.

The Nomads were an elite group of children that lived and trained in this compound. They were soldiers, each and every one of them, though the official records would probably never say so. No, according to the little bit of paperwork Steven had glimpsed on occasion, the Special Operators Group and Nomad Task Force were classified as an advanced after-school ROTC program that included basic martial arts and weapon safety training.

A man, General Darius Blackwood, brought Steven—at the time, an eight-year-old orphan—to Blue Rock. There were originally about twenty of them altogether. Until the previous year, that was. Steven wondered how they had actually covered up what had to be three deaths in the course of a few weeks.

He hadn't seen the other two bodies, but would never forget the image of the four-inch tactical knife sunk into one girl's chest. There were no leads, and the official story in each case was that the children had been found and taken in by family. Steven understood then that only a fool could believe the official stories.

2 Young Blood

Emily always hated the scents of the gymnasium. It smelled of floor polish, rubber, and sweat. Since childhood, she associated those scents with the day her mother died. It should have just been a hard day, filled with the difficulties of simple bullying in physical education class. But the evening that started with her crying to her mother about the older kids picking on her, had ended with Emily clutching a lifeless corpse as her brother stood over them with their mom's gun, having shot the intruders.

She shook her head to clear the memory, wishing she could feel the heat from the light coming in through windows set high in the wall. The sunlight cut the harsh glare from unnatural halogen bulbs lining the ceiling. Emily held a tattered novel, wishing without hope that she could just while the day away reading.

General Blackwood escorted them into the bright room as though they'd never been there before. Captain Abaroa's gaze fell on the Nomads from the other end of the gym. Emily hated evaluation days more than the smell of the gym. Although, on a less primal level.

Captain Abaroa stood by with another young man--Steven-- on one of the martial arts pads. The familiar scar on Steven's chest shone like a beacon through the sweat-soaked white t-shirt. The jagged pink line of it reminded her of a bloody stream.

Abaroa snapped, "Break time's over. Drop. Twenty."

Steven dropped into the pushups, counting with each repetition. Abaroa barked again, and Steven leaped to his feet and ran around the track surrounding the gym. He transitioned smoothly, but robotically.

"Cross, you have command," Blackwood said dryly, glaring down at Joseph.

Joseph called out. "Conditioning Drill Two. Stow personal items and be on the mat in three minutes."

Emily rolled her eyes and stifled a groan. Out of the three conditioning drills, Emily could always count on full-contact sparring following Conditioning Drill Two.

This just keeps getting better. And, how the hell does Steven fit into the evaluation?

She kept half an eye on Steven over the top of her novel. His presence was an idle mystery. He only got placed in training with the Nomads when Abaroa or one of the others in command wanted to punish him for something. She thought about some of the things Blackwood's thugs did to her the last time she 'stepped out of line', and shuddered.

Maurice smiled, offering his hand. "Want me to take that for you?"

She handed him the novel, its frayed pages seeming to reach up to caress her fingers as she let go. He jogged over to the nearby bleachers, where he placed both the novel and his messenger bag. Then, the Nomads assembled in line and began their normal exercise regimen. A hundred each of push-ups, sit-ups, and pull-ups. Steven finished his tenth lap, marking a mile, and snapped into the routine with them without a word.

Blackwood and Abaroa stepped away, walking out of earshot. Emily startled at Abaroa's proud expression as Blackwood gestured, red-faced and staring pointedly at Steven. Emily hated the slickly unpleasant coating of sweat beginning to form along her body.

What the hell did the dumbass do this time?

Joseph called a halt after a solid half-hour, allowed them a few minutes to stretch, then ordered a run. Emily felt invigorated. Her pulse pounded its familiar rhythm. And again, Steven kept up with them. Steven faltered when they neared the end of the mile run.

His second mile run. I swear he's part machine.

Joseph raised a hand, halting their run. "Ten minutes, Nomads."

Joseph always stood out with his buzz-cut hair the color of burnished copper. Like her own tightly pulled ponytail. Joseph's dark hazel eyes found her as they sat on the bleachers. He chuckled as he tilted his head at Steven, who moved over to a wall, and sat scowling at the Nomads.

Maurice reached into the bag beside him and pulled his usual device from it. He strapped it to his wrist and started playing with icons on the screen. He looked up at her with a smile.

"I'm updating the databrace firmware," he said, turning his attention back to his toy. "R&D says they want to integrate it into the HUD on the armor today."

Emily opened her novel. "So, they finally got those rust traps working right? I'm pretty sure I broke a rib breathing last time we tested it."

Maurice gestured with a hand, absently waving the databrace. "You pushed it too far, Emily. It amplifies movement by a significant degree. I told you to take it easy. But I guess we'll see if it's ready tomorrow after breakfast."

Maurice perked up as if having an afterthought as he continued to tinker. "Word has it Lieutenant Petrovic finished some kind of advancement to a couple of the rifles, too."

Emily twirled a finger in the air sarcastically and turned back to focus on her novel. The cover hung on by threads, and the yellowed pages crinkled every time she turned them. After a few moments, she felt a touch on her leg. She stared at Antoine's offending hand, shoved it away, and moved to another bench. She looked back at Antoine's angular face, stretched in a predatory cat-eyed grin.

She felt a little better when she glanced at Nikifor, his ever-watchful eyes glued to Antoine. He whispered something to Joseph. Joseph spun and grabbed Antoine by the shirt, pulling the other young man in close. He hissed some sort of murderous threat Emily couldn't hear from her new perch. When Joseph let go, Antoine swallowed hard and clenched his fists.

While they rested, Emily read the small, tattered novel in silence. A slight movement caught her eye, and she looked up to see Steven standing in front of Joseph. Staring at him with arms crossed.

"What do you want, puke?" demanded Joseph, his expression unflinching.

Steven shrugged. "I'm ready for the spar. I have homework. Let's get this over with."

Joseph raised an eyebrow. "You realize there's a reason for the separation between our units."

"I've seen you guys spar before. I think I've got a handle on how each of you fights. You're the most dangerous. I'm not ready for you, and I recognize that. But, except for those two," Steven pointed at Nikifor and Emily, "the rest of these guys are trying to think of a way to beat you. Those two already have their plan. Somehow, I feel it won't be enough."

"Those two are too scared of you to be a challenge," Steven said, pointing to Maurice and Antoine. He finally pointed at Valko's square face. "And he's too angry to beat you."

"Piss off, kid," laughed Antoine. "You have no idea-"

"You're the most afraid of him," said Steven, glancing at Antoine impassively. "The weakest dogs always bark the loudest."

Antoine jumped up, but Joseph put a hand on his chest, stopping him.

Joseph smiled. "You got balls, kid. Tell you what. I'll give you a one-on-one with Country Mile here. Before I let him kick your ass, though, what's your name again?"

"Steven."

"Steven, huh?" said Joseph, seemingly digesting the name. He dropped his hand from Antoine's chest. "Cool. Looks like the rest of us have a few more minutes."

Emily closed the book momentarily as the two of them stood opposite each other in the middle of the mats. Even though they had performed the conditioning workouts together before, this would be the first time Steven sparred with any of them. She wanted to see how he would fight. Antoine beat Steven in weight class alone, by at least thirty pounds, and towered over him. Oh, the difference a couple of years in age could make in a person's build. Joseph gave the signal, and Antoine rushed forward. Steven dropped to the floor and kicked up into Antoine's crotch.

Antoine doubled over with a loud whine. Abaroa and Blackwood looked stunned, turning their attention to the battle. Steven performed a kip-up and hopped into a spin kick, catching Antoine in the side of the head.

Does he think he's Jackie Chan or something? That was pointless!

Steven followed with a short flurry of punches to Antoine's face and neck. Antoine staggered back. He shook his head and then struck Steven with a backhand sending Steven sliding across the floor.

Steven groaned as he struggled to his feet. The empty look in his eyes made Emily shiver. She recognized that darkness. That point she sometimes reached where the numbness took over and she fought just to feel something real. He threw a feint, earning a nod from Nikifor. Antoine twitched a block to one side. Steven followed with several punches and a kick, landing them on Antoine's face and torso. Antoine stumbled again, face red. He kicked out, catching Steven in the stomach.

Steven crumpled, groaning. He put his weight on his hands but couldn't lift himself from the floor. His body shook. No sound came out. Antoine kicked him again, dropping him completely.

Nikifor got up. "If you're not calling this, Cross, I am. Steven's done."

Joseph signaled for Antoine to stop. And Antoine kicked again. Emily raised an eyebrow. Defying Joseph? Considering whatever threat Joseph leveled after Antoine touched her, Antoine must be getting suicidal. Nikifor shoved Antoine away and helped Steven over to his spot by the wall. Emily's gaze lingered on Steven's glistening dark, empty eyes. His face resembled a statue in the rain, haunting her.

"Hey," said Nikifor, placing a gentle hand on Steven's shoulder. "You tried, and your best wasn't enough. It happens. This won't help, but you were close to beating him. You did good."

The more she thought about it, the more Emily recognized the truth in Nikifor's words. Steven must have baited Antoine on purpose. Maurice wouldn't have been enough of a challenge by himself. But Steven and Antoine were more evenly matched than she initially understood. She recognized the look in his eyes. The frustration. Those tears. She knew the pain far too well. Too much like every time she got into the ring with Joseph, the broken bones and dislocated joints were a pale prize against the backdrop of trying to push beyond her limits.

"The hell?" yelled Antoine. "I could kick your ass, too!"

"Shut up." Joseph glared, arms crossed. Antoine withered, protectively clutching at the side of his head and his crotch.

"Steven broke through that piss-poor defense of yours before you knew you got hit. Would have beat you with another solid hit or two. Webb could knock you out in his sleep. Hell, I'd take the puke over your cowardly ass any day, but it's not my decision. Now our entertainment's over, let's get this done so we can eat. I'd like to not miss dinner today."

Joseph's order couldn't have been clearer. Emily put her book back on the bench, then stood, and moved to the center of the gym floor. They all gathered, shuffling into position around Joseph. Steven watched from his spot near the wall, his dark eyes like wet stones, bright red welts forming on his body.

Emily hated how much Steven's assessment captured the reality of their situation. Joseph called himself Cross. She supposed, not for the first time, he meant it to be a representation of painful finality for anyone facing him. That it was their last name was probably just a lovely bonus to him. Joseph watched his opponents, adapting to their movements. If one of them could catch him off guard, maybe land one or two lucky blows, it might not go so poorly as almost every other time. He held his spot as the leader of the Nomads through sheer willpower.

Valko moved in to grab him, but Joseph spun to the side allowing him to pass, then planted a kick to the back of Valko's knee. Joseph launched himself into another spin, punching into Antoine's collarbone. A muffled pop resonated from Antoine's shoulder, and he screamed in pain. Joseph turned and executed a roundhouse kick, catching Maurice in the temple, dropping him to the floor.

Emily seized the moment, getting into position while Joseph looked off-balance. Nikifor moved at the same time, jumping forward with a kick. Emily threw a punch. Joseph dodged, but the kick hit him in the shoulder, spinning him to one side. Joseph controlled his spin, whirling with a powerful step. He made use of his momentum to launch a straight kick into Emily's gut. She felt the air rush from her mouth as the blow lifted her off the mat. She lay on the floor spluttering, as Nikifor swung, catching Joseph in the chest. While she struggled to breathe, Emily watched as Nikifor, Maurice, and Valko rushed in; Nikifor from behind, Valko from in front, Maurice from the side.

Valko slammed into Joseph's torso as Nikifor ducked to sweep his legs from under him. Joseph smiled as he fell, Maurice's attack sailing over harmlessly. Valko adjusted his grip, following him to the ground. Joseph struck out with an elbow on the way, hitting Nikifor in the temple. Nikifor dropped to the floor, dazed.

Valko straddled Joseph and drove his fist down. Joseph deflected the blow and hit him in the throat. Joseph followed up with a punch to the jaw, knocking Valko off and to the mat. There were stars in Emily's vision as she finally pulled in a breath and stood, but she watched as Maurice tried to kick down at Joseph and got kicked in the crotch for the effort.

Joseph got to his feet as Emily darted in and threw an easily deflected jab, followed closely by an uppercut, catching Joseph on the chin. He kicked out, pushing her back. She threw another punch toward his head. Joseph stepped into the blow, pulling her punching arm further as he wrapped her head in a lock. He yanked her down and brought his knee into her gut. Her entire body exploded in pain. Her vision went black for several seconds.

The cold floor was little relief to her pounding head. As much as she hated to admit it, they were done. She tried to catch her breath, but her lungs wouldn't fill. What few breaths she gathered came in quick and shallow bursts, but each successful intake of oxygen felt like a miraculous gift. Not even a ten-minute spar and they were done. Antoine would have to get his shoulder reset. A minor punishment, considering his act of insubordination. And the rest of them would nurse some new bruises for the night. It never really seemed to matter, though. The experimental medicines would take care of the issue in a few days.

Two medics strode calmly into the room, assessing injuries while Blackwood stood to the side of the ring, a dark-clad monolith. He glared at Steven, who still sat by the wall.

"I've made a decision," said Blackwood, as the medics finished applying a cold compress to Antoine's shoulder. "The final roster for Nomad training will be Joseph, Nikifor, Valko, Maurice, and Antoine. Emily is being transferred out of the program."

"That's bull-," yelled Joseph. "Emily's earned her spot, just like the rest of us. She's a better candidate than Antoine."

Blackwood's eyes grew dark, his tone commanding. "Don't presume to instruct me on what I'm looking for in this unit. The decision is made, and she's being transferred to another facility. Is that understood?"

Joseph almost growled the words, "Yes, sir."

Blackwood turned on his heel and walked away, the sound of his boots receding through the gym. Nikifor looked at her apologetically, but Emily waved it off as she walked away.

Emily went into the girl's locker room, putting the combination into her lock. She pulled the elastic band from her hair, letting the sweat-soaked red locks tumble down around her shoulders, slammed her novel into the locker and sighed. Closing it, she pressed her forehead into the cold, tan-painted steel, trying to wrap her head around what just happened. She undressed and took a towel from the rack beside the lockers.

On a whim, Emily glanced at one of the other lockers. She could swear she could still see the blood on it, even through the several layers of paint covering it. Emily hadn't known the other girl long enough to really grow to miss her, but finding the body was enough of a shock; the images of it seared themselves into her nightmares.

Emily padded to the shower area and turned on the water. She stood under the spray, hoping the heat would comfort her and calm her racing heartbeat. Her skin turned red from the scalding water. Some days, the pain from the water cresting over her body, searing into new cuts and bruises turned out to be the only thing keeping her sane. Especially in this facility. Her novels described a world unknown to her for almost ten years. She listened to the hollow patter of the artificial storm pouring over her. A sound out of sync with the falling water caught her attention.

A spike of panic seized her. Still slick with soap, she turned, wiping her eyes. Antoine stared at her, a vicious grin twisting his lips. He maneuvered the cloth sling from around his reset shoulder and stretched the arm. Aside from this, he only wore a towel around his waist. He put a finger to his lips.

She ignored the initial rush of adrenaline telling her to punch him in the ugly bruise growing on his shoulder.

"Shh," he said, moving forward with cat-like steps. "Since you're leaving soon, I thought we'd have a little fun. Shall we?"

"Get out," Emily said firmly, her eyes fixed on him. She didn't doubt the violence in his eyes. It spoke to her on a primal level. Her heart raced, as she considered the situation.

So he wants to make good on those veiled threats? I guess I wounded his pride enough.

She centered her thoughts, breathing as deeply as she dared, willing her heart to slow as she forced herself to stand without a tremor, showing a fearlessness she didn't feel. She wondered whether she should punch him in the throat; or should she go for the shoulder first? A dark thought occurred to her. Should she accidentally kill him, it might get her spot back. The realization brought a smile to her face.

His grin widened. He unwrapped the towel from his waist, stopping a moment to let her 'admire' the view. Emily stared into his eyes impassively until his face became a stiff mask of violent intent. He dropped his hands to his sides. Even naked, she would not allow him to make her cower.

"And here I thought I was bein' nice. Y'know? Givin' you a chance to have a little fun before you go. Is this how it's gonna be?"

Her pulse remained fast and steady, but the indignity of it all forced Emily to return his icy stare. "Either you turn around and walk out, or someone will drag your body out."

"We'll see." He dropped the towel, revealing a small knife hidden in a fold.

Antoine lunged, swinging the knife. Emily stepped back and slipped, stumbling. Her elbow slammed into the shower's steel knob, and pain shot through her arm. He followed with a second swing, her blood spraying as the blade bit in just underneath her breast. Emily clenched her teeth to bury as much of the pained grunt as she could.

Enraged, Emily grabbed his arm and yanked with all her strength. The look of surprise on his face made the now skin-to-skin contact feel worth it as Antoine's face smacked into the tiled shower wall. Dark blood dripped onto her skin, warm and slick. She slammed the arm still in her grasp into the fixture. He dropped the knife in the water, now running with streams of red from their blood.

Antoine clenched his teeth and punched into her gut. She barely blocked, the impact sending more shooting pain through her arm and chest. He reached out with the other hand and grabbed her by the throat, lifting her off the floor.

Emily saw red. Instead of fighting the grapple, she rammed a knuckle into the center of his throat. He dropped her and clutched his throat, choking. Emily kicked into the side of his knee, cringing at the wet smack of his face on the concrete floor.

He rose a little, shaking his head. She drove her heel into his chest. A distinct crunch sounded from his ribs, and he collapsed, coughing blood onto the floor. Antoine scrambled away, dragging himself by his good arm. She laughed at the mixture of fear and hatred in his eyes. He curled into a fetal position against the wall and coughed more blood.

"I don't think you understand," said Emily, finally turning off the water. She grabbed her towel from its hook near the shower and fixed it around her body. Crouching down, she grabbed the knife. "I will kill you to get my spot back. You just gave me the justification."

Nikifor and Joseph ran into the shower room as she approached Antoine with his potential death playing in her mind.

"Seriously?" said Joseph, spitting on Antoine's curled form. "I thought I told you to stay away from my sister."

Antoine's eyes widened as he groaned, and he spluttered nervously. "We were just gonna have a little fun, ya know?"

"Oh, shut up," said Joseph. He glanced over, his eyes darkened, becoming murderous as they moved across the blood that had survived being washed away. He dropped a steel-toed boot onto Antoine's recently reset shoulder. A sound like the cracking of dried wood echoed in the room. Antoine went rigid and howled. Joseph kicked him again.

"I had this handled," said Emily, an exasperated sigh escaping.

Joseph didn't look up. "Like I care."

She put a hand to her head. "You literally...whatever, could you three just get out now? This is already more awkward than it needs to be."

Nikifor moved forward, placing a hand on Joseph's shoulder as he lifted his boot for another kick. Joseph stopped and put his foot down.

"Whatever," said Joseph as he shrugged Nikifor's hand off and stomped out.

Nikifor grabbed Antoine's towel, draping it around the other young man's waist. Nikifor held his hand out to Emily. She rolled her eyes and placed the knife in his hand. He considered for a moment before folding the small blade, pinning the edges of the towel together.

"You believe me, don't you?" Antoine pleaded.

Nikifor looked into Antoine's eyes and spoke quietly. "You were warned. Be thankful you're alive. I only wish we were a few seconds slower. Learn from this moment. Become a better man."

The things he said resonated with the sound of running water. He grabbed Antoine by the broken shoulder, eliciting a howl as he squeezed the broken bones and hefted.

Emily shuddered. Something about Nikifor's cold anger scared her more than any of the others. The way he could look at a person, and seemingly see their hidden selves. She crossed her arms, blocking an unsettled shiver as she found meaning in his glare. He hoped she would have killed Antoine, as well. The opportunity was lost on their arrival. Her shoulders slumped at her conflicted thoughts.

I was too slow. No wonder they're sending me away.

Without looking at her, Nikifor nodded as Antoine finally fell unconscious from the pain.

"Thanks, Spock," said Emily, using her fingers to pinch too tightly at her sides. "Why is it you seem to be the only person here who actually understands what people need?"

"Who knows." Nikifor shrugged. A small, warm smile played across his lips as he shouldered the unconscious Antoine and carried him from the shower room. That smile relieved her.

It wasn't until the next day when she got loaded into some woman's car and driven away from the Blue Rock Arsenal, that she considered the reality of her situation. Of course, the report about Antoine's assault on her got swept under the rug.

Either way, everything was over. She was done with the whole experience. No more lab work. No more needles. No more screaming in the night, wishing for an end to pains she should never have felt.

She reflexively felt for the Vindicator revolver holstered in the rear of her waistband. She'd stolen it from the requisitions officer the night before. The weight of the gun, like her training, was all the security she'd need going forward. She turned away from her novel long enough to watch the concrete facade of the building fade into the city. One day, she'd return. If only to watch it burn to the ground.

<u>3 Infection</u>

Steven entered his homeroom the morning after training, rubbing sore muscles. His face warmed at the still-fresh memory of Antoine's beating. He knew Antoine wasn't exactly the weakest fighter of their little special club, but he hadn't figured it would be quite so one-sided.

Steven gave it everything and received nothing but the bruises in return. Maybe he should have gone for the weakest-looking one. Maurice? But no. He'd wanted the challenge. He'd wanted to push his limits. The sound of students laughing and greeting each other drowned his thoughts.

Steven paused in the classroom doorway. Dr. Wayde Harper sat at his desk with a Captain America comic book open in his hands. And, though appearing to be engaged with his comic book, Steven had paused under the gaze of the teacher's critical eyes.

Harper's silvery hair swept back from his face like a lion's mane. To Steven, Dr. Harper looked like a stereotype of the 1980s, wearing a black shirt with some obscure, but probably funny—to him—equation on the front. He also had on black high-top sneakers—propped up on his desk—black slacks, and a brown belt with a buckle shaped like a trout eating the leather band.

"Wonderful morning today, isn't it, Mr. Fuller? I have a question for you," said Dr. Harper, putting down his comic book. It showed an image of Captain America bleeding out from a bullet hole, lying on a set of concrete steps with his hands bound behind his back. Steven forced his gaze away from the image, eyes landing on Dr. Harper's wide grin.

"Have you ever wondered about human nature? About what it is?"

Steven shrugged. "Not really. I get what I expect from people. That's enough."

Harper raised an eyebrow, pointedly looking at Steven's bandaged hands. "I suppose you think you have a point."

"Are you saying I'm wrong about what I've gotten from people?"

"Not at all," said Harper. "What I'm saying is that you have an idea in your mind about what to expect from people, but you're not considering what human nature is."

Steven rolled his eyes and moved from the doorway. Harper held up a finger, and he stopped.

Great. He wants to wax philosophically again.

The other students in the room stilled and began to listen. Some appeared to be genuinely considering the question. Others took the opportunity to point and giggle at Dr. Harper's victim. It seemed to be their favorite part of class when Dr. Harper would catch some unwitting student on their way in the door with some unanswerable question. Not always Steven, but usually Steven.

"Okay," Steven groaned. "What is human nature?"

"Ah," said Dr. Harper, raising a finger and rising to his feet, animated. "That's the question, isn't it? People claim every day that the things they engage in are a part of their human nature." He'd said 'human nature' while gesturing in air quotes.

"So, you're saying all those people are wrong?"

Harper smiled. "What I'm saying is, human nature is an undefinable trait. I could tell you, with all my conviction, that eating healthy and exercising are just human nature. After all, it is how our ancestors survived long enough to start our family lines, isn't it? I could say all people born under the Gemini constellation are adaptable or impulsive. But does it become true?"

Steven shrugged.

"Most people are adaptable and impulsive," said Dr. Harper, louder. On a roll, so to speak. "Because those are human survival mechanisms. And yet, people try to pigeonhole themselves into these little...categories."

He put an airy, nasal sound into his voice. "Oh, I'm a Shoehorn Crab, because I was born under the full moon on a leap year. My horoscope says I'm highly intelligent, but intelligence can make me unreliable and nosy."

Dr. Harper's antics elicited laughter from the classroom, and he bounded to the chalkboard. He cleared his throat.

"So, I ask again. This time, any of you can answer. What is the nature of humanity? What is human nature?"

Steven trudged to his seat, sighing in relief, as several students called out answers, some more ridiculous than others. One girl actually said some of the same crap Dr. Harper mocked. Although Dr. Harper was animated and engaging--as usual--something shone in his eyes today. Some wild, feral energy Steven couldn't place. Harper's eyes had a slightly puffy and bloodshot look to them.

Harper's black t-shirt darkened in places from sweat. The man's forehead glistened as he raved on about the banality of both the American and Asian zodiacs.

Is this guy drunk? High?

Steven tuned out the raving class, choosing instead to doodle in his sketch pad. The drawings weren't any good, even when his hands weren't stinging from damage. But it kept his hands busy. He vaguely wondered at how much better his hands felt, considering the abuse they'd gone through the day before but got distracted trying to figure out why he kept squirming in his seat.

In a sudden start, Steven noticed what he'd drawn: a man lying on his back in a pool of blood. Steven slammed his sketchpad shut to get away from the image of his dead father.

Someone whispered, "Why is he such a freak?"

"Yeah...total psycho, bro. He straight-up destroyed Curtis in the cafeteria yesterday. I heard he almost killed him."

Steven didn't care enough to respond. *It never even got that far.* They probably didn't think anyone could hear them over the excited chattering of the other students.

His eyes flickered with constant motion, casing the room for points of escape, landing finally on his backpack. He swallowed his feelings and calmed his heart rate. It wouldn't do him any good to panic for no real reason.

But what was that manic look in Dr. Harper's eyes? He looked so proud of his philosophical quandary. A simple question with a complicated answer. What the hell was so special about that?

He lifted the backpack as the bell began to peal. Steven jostled and slipped along through the halls. Most of the morning went predictably. He turned in papers for his English and Biology classes. He almost dozed through Algebra, since rifle training included a crash course in trigonometry, algebra, and calculus.

Soon enough, the bell sounded for lunch. Steven went through the line and grabbed a milk, an apple, and what the school called a chicken sandwich. He navigated the tables until he found his favorite one. Sitting in the chair, he could keep his back to everything and watch birds play out in the school's courtyard.

He took a bite of the sandwich and regretted it. Out of the corner of his eye, he caught Grace and Mirena making their way over from the lunch line. They chattered excitedly, Grace grinning with a blush, and Mirena waving her arms about.

Great. Grace probably told her everything about the previous day's conversation.

The sandwich stuck to the roof of his mouth in protest to the provided milk and tasted remarkably like drywall covered with a layer of bread. The ketchup didn't help, either. He chuckled to himself as he wished for something else on the bread.

Not so much a sandwich, as a sand-wish.

He gave up on it. Setting the sandwich back on the tray, he slid the thing to the side and bent over to reach into his backpack. Hands closed over his eyes and a soft chest pressed into his back.

"Guess who," said the lightly accented voice. She was being intentionally breathy, the warmth tickling his neck. His face flushed with color, but he buried the embarrassment quickly. Envious banter from other guys in the cafeteria floated to him over the din of the crowd. He inwardly cringed. She was way too good at making a spectacle.

Attempting to remain polite and sociable, Steven braced himself to play along. He said, "Same bat time, same bat channel. If it isn't the dynamic duo, Mirepoix and Sylvester!"

Steven gave a half-hearted attempt at sounding surprised, and the two girls laughed at his fake gasp. Mirena took her hands from his eyes and wrapped them around his neck. She pressed in just a little harder.

Grace moved to sit at the other side of the table and rolled her eyes playfully. Steven couldn't decide if she was reacting to his comments or Mirena's behavior. Probably both, in all honesty.

"Mirena," she whispered in his ear, "Mee-ray-nah." She released him and gave him a playful little push. "And, the blonde is Grace, Esteban. How many times have I got to tell you?"

Grace grinned. "Sufferin' succotash! Leave him be, Mirena. It's hard enough to eat looking at you. But seriously, watching you throw yourself at the guy I'm trying to take to the dance is nauseating."

Steven shook his head, trying to fight the rising heat in his cheeks. He retrieved an MRE from his backpack. Sitting up, he grinned and shrugged as Mirena sat down next to Steven, rolling her eyes with a shake of the head, poking her tongue out at Grace in a juvenile manner.

"Well, now I'm sitting by your guy," Mirena intoned as she reached across Steven, brushing into him, and snatched his abandoned sandwich. Mirena's complex-looking silver earring flashed in his face as her deep brown hair caressed him.

Grace raised an eyebrow, her cheeks red. She glared daggers at her cousin. Grace straightened in her chair. She hissed something Steven didn't catch. In response, Mirena laughed and did a little wiggle in the chair, pointing at her chest.

"Who knows?" he said, intentionally ignoring the exchange between the girls, "Maybe I'll get your names right someday. Or you'll get tired of telling me. That's the one I'm really hoping for."

The three of them laughed as Steven tore open the packaging on his meal. Mirena bit into the purloined sandwich. Grace unwrapped her own.

Mirena waved the half-eaten torture between bread. "So, what's on the menu, since you ain't finishing this slop?"

Steven looked at the packaging in his hand. He hadn't checked before he'd packed it. Looking at it now, he wished he had looked at it. He made a face.

"Let's see…shredded barbecue beef, tortilla with cheese spread, and trail mix. Complemented with powdered lime drink and freeze-dried coffee."

Both of the girls made a face, too, once he got to the drinks. He pulled a water bottle from the side pocket of his backpack.

"It's not as bad as it sounds. I mean, it beats the hell out of that cement sandwich."

He smiled at Mirena's look of indignation as she tried to talk around the mouthful of dry chicken. He tore open the accessory pack and tossed her a packet of barbecue sauce.

"I'm just saying, you're gonna need this more than I will."

Steven opened the freeze-dried coffee packet and poured it into his water bottle, shaking it. The brown powder chunks became black coffee. He took a sip of the bitter black liquid, grateful for a flavor only somewhat less like chalk than the sandwich. *Chalky liquid beats chalky sandwich any day.* Then, he ripped open the main course bag and grabbed his fork, tucking in.

"Hol' up, nene," said Mirena. "You're eating that cold?"

"What'd you call me, and why did you call me that?"

"Nene," said Mirena, "it means baby boy. You trying to tell us something, Steven? I could've sworn you were a boy."

"You are, quite literally, the only person in my life to ever call me that."

Mirena grinned her sneaky, sultry smile, "Maybe I should take you home to Puerto Rico. Mama would love you. I'm sure she'd call you nene for a while, too. At least, until we make it official." She waggled her ring finger in his face.

"You may want to check with Grace first." Steven shrugged as he took another bite.

It would have taken at least fifteen minutes for the flameless ration heater to warm it, and you couldn't exactly put the thing in a microwave. Even if he could convince the teachers to let him use either one of those items. They hovered around the thing almost as much as the water cooler.

The meat tasted moister than the sandwich he'd given up on. Not too bad on flavor, either, honestly. Why he kept trying to swallow down the swill the school called lunch, he couldn't figure out. Maybe someday they'd learn how to make a decent meal. Grace looked at him with a raised eyebrow. He had trouble interpreting the look.

Grace said, "Could I try a bite?"

He held out a forkful of the red mush. She took it, throwing a satisfied sidelong glance at Mirena as she bit in. Her face scrunched.

"That is," she said, shaking her head as she handed the fork back and took a sip of the soda she'd brought, "not what I expected."

Steven shrugged again. He'd been eating MREs since before he'd come to Blue Rock. His father had introduced him to them while struggling to learn how to cook. Thinking about it still made his chest feel tight–made his eyes feel warm. He cleared his throat and took another bite. Grace became quiet.

"Did I say something wrong? You look upset."

Steven smiled, soft and sad. "It's not that. Don't worry about it."

"So," said Mirena, taking another bite of sand-wish, "Grace asked you out yesterday, I hear."

"Yeah?" said Steven. "What of it?"

Mirena glared at him. "Are you taking her to the dance or not? You gotta tell her, or she'll be pestering me to ask you all the time."

Grace looked incredulous, "I will not!"

Steven forced a smile. "I'm not telling you. I'll tell Grace in class and let her pester you with the answer."

Steven finished eating moments before the end of lunch bell rang. He rose, grabbed his backpack, and nodded at the girls. As he made his way through the halls, a gentle hand touched his elbow. He turned toward the touch, his gaze landing on Grace's thoughtful hazel eyes.

"You're still upset," said Grace.

Steven cursed under his breath. Was it really so obvious?

"Sorry," said Steven. "I was thinking about my dad."

Grace nodded. "I see. You don't really talk about him much."

They walked for a few moments in silence, approaching the art room's door. Steven hesitated, but walked through and settled at the desk before he spoke again.

He said, "It's not easy to talk about."

Grace settled across from him. "I understand. I won't bug you if you don't want to talk about it."

Mr. Sorensen started coughing across the room. Every hair on Steven's body stood on end as something like a cold shock burst in his chest. Sorensen's arms were bulging, and he held a hand to his chest. The ragged coughing sounded far too wet. His skin reddened, and he coughed blood onto his desk. Steven couldn't tell from the distance, but the color of the blood seemed a strange, dark shade of red. Mr. Sorensen's pencil-thin arms getting suddenly muscular struck something within that Steven couldn't name.

Steven's instincts screamed at him to stay away. Students gasped and screamed. In fact, Steven could swear there were screams from other classrooms as well.

Grace started to move, but Steven grabbed her by the arm before she could go to Mr. Sorensen.

"Let go," she said, panicked. "He needs help!"

"No." He grabbed his backpack with his other hand, adrenaline coursing through tired veins. "We need to go."

She struggled against his grip as others around them panicked. There was fury in her eyes as she freed herself. He needed to remember his training. Remain calm. The two guys Steven recognized from the football team reached Mr. Sorensen first. One of them grabbed Sorensen by the shoulder.

Mr. Sorensen spun at them, catching one of the boys with a blow that snapped his neck to the side awkwardly. The other stopped short as his friend dropped to the tile floor, but Sorensen's other hand shot out, impaling the young man's face with his fingers. A moment later, Sorensen pulled his hand back, revealing long claws extending from his fingers, and let the body drop.

Grace clasped hands over her mouth as she retreated. Steven placed himself between her and the carnage. Several gunshots overcut the noise of screaming. The sound came from close by. Somewhere within the building.

Steven breathed deep, preparing himself, as screaming students pushed and ran around him and Grace. Getting trampled would be bad. Being caught by one of Sorensen's clawed hands would be worse. Steven needed to time it so Grace wouldn't get dragged down or attacked in the shuffle.

More shots. Sorensen's head turned from side to side, slowly scanning the room. He lifted a claw to his face and appeared to sniff it. The sound eerily similar to an animal sampling the smell of new, unfamiliar food. Sorensen's eyes widened, and he licked at the blood coating a claw, snuffling as he went. Sorensen turned his attention to Steven and eyed him curiously for a few moments. His lips twisted in a snarling grin.

Grace sobbed, with hands held tightly to her mouth. Steven had to get her out of this hell, but it would be close. Sorensen made too big of a step in their direction and slipped in the blood pooling at his feet. He glared at his feet as though they'd betrayed him. Sorensen got his feet back under him and lunged forward. Blood flew from the claws as he opened his arms wide, teeth bared, face filled with animalistic anger.

Steven would have shot him, but everything was happening so fast, he hadn't thought to grab his gun yet. So, he settled for the next best option. Steven kicked a chair into Sorensen's path, causing the mutated teacher to stumble and sprawl across the floor. Warm droplets of blood splashed on Steven's face from the monster's flailing fall. Steven shoved Grace toward the door. He wondered again at the gunshots he'd heard, but survival came first.

They ran.

Grace screamed over the noise. "What the hell is going on, Steven? What are these things?"

"I don't know," he said, pulling her forward. "It's like a bad movie or something. But I've got you. I'll get you out of this."

Steven and Grace moved as quickly as they could through the crowd of panicked students. He glanced into a classroom on the way down the hall and regretted it. A mutated teacher held a broken body in its claws. Steven pushed ahead as it dropped the body and turned, glaring about the room.

He ignored the crashes and screams coming through the closed door of the second-floor teacher's lounge. Eventually, they came to one of the staircases leading down to the ground floor.

"Mirena's in math class, right?"

Grace shuddered, a mute nod her only response.

Steven stopped a moment and dropped his backpack. Opening it, he reached into the hidden pocket behind his books and retrieved the Glock 26 subcompact pistol and its magazine.

"Why do you have a gun?" said Grace, eyes wide and voice rising in pitch.

"For when I need it." Steven readied the weapon.

"Look," he said, "We'll discuss this. I promise I'll tell you everything. For right now, just let me finish saving you."

A door down the hall behind them burst from its hinges as a taloned monster tackled a running student and stabbed them with claws made of bone. Steven pushed Grace into the stairwell, and they descended. Entering the ground floor hallway, they passed by the office. The body of one of the office ladies slumped against the wall, half covering a smear of blood; a dark, bloody hole in her shirt.

"What the hell?" said Steven, sweeping the area even more cautiously than before.

Grace groaned. "What now?"

"She's not mutated, but someone shot her."

"How many people are running around this school with guns?"

Steven thought for a long moment as they moved through the rushing stream of people. Not everyone would have been as prepared as him. They kept making that clear in training. Obsessive, they called him. Paranoid, claimed others. But there were a few who took him seriously.

"Counting me, maybe five?"

Grace huffed. "Great."

They continued against the flow of fleeing students. Thankfully, the way wasn't as difficult, as the hallways were emptying quickly. Steven and Grace picked up speed just beyond where they would turn to go to the cafeteria. The silence of the hallway concerned him, but they needed to keep moving. They came to a closed classroom door, and Steven ripped the door open.

Smashed desks. Blood and bodies. A small knot of survivors huddled in the corner. Where was Mirena? The former teacher, kneeling just inside the door on a body, turned. Her misshapen mouth dripped saliva and blood. She snarled, clicking her talons on the floor. A movement from beneath the teacher's desk caught his and the monster's attention. Mirena's head poked around, tear streaks through her makeup. There was a thin ribbon of blood running from her forehead down her cheek.

Grace dashed around Steven, startling him as she grabbed for Mirena. The monster lunged for them. *If I shoot and miss, I'll hit one of the other students.*

Steven ran forward, kicking the monster hard in its side. It swiped out with a claw as he pressed in further. The claws passed by, but the force of the blow knocked him over. Steven rolled to his feet, jumped onto a desk, and aimed. He fired two shots into the monster's face. The pops of the pistol seemed to bounce off the walls of the room, reverberating as the pistol recoiled into his hand.

The sound of the room settled until Steven could hear something besides the heartbeat pounding in his ears. Steven glanced around the room at students with covered ears. Grace and Mirena were safe. He was alive. He debated how to get them home. He felt a vibration in his pocket and pulled out the cell phone. It was Abaroa. Steven stared at his screen for a few heartbeats more.

4 Welcome To The War

Miles away from Arkansas, and the woman Emily was riding with just wouldn't stop talking. They were somewhere in Tennessee at the moment, but the highway seemed to stretch forever onward. Emily had been hearing facts and figures about the group home for hours. The more she heard, the more it sounded like what she'd just left behind. Only, this time, she wouldn't be free to punch the people who got on her nerves.

Where are we even going? It's dark as hell out here.

The woman pulled into a spot at a combination gas station, truck stop, and roadside diner. The small parking lot held a loose scattering of cars, trucks, and minivans. Impressive, considering it was close to midnight. Emily mused at the austerity of the highway system.

She'd read about it more than seen it, but it was a military project from looks alone. Information came on a need-to-know basis. Someone could cross from one side of the country to the other without seeing anything noteworthy.

"Come on, then, dear," said the woman. "Let's stretch our legs and get something to eat. You are hungry, aren't you?"

Emily considered rolling her eyes but decided to go along with it. "Sure."

Five guys wearing black and blue bandanas stood around a dark, indigo-colored SUV, laughing. The glint of their jewelry was too bright in the reflection of the truck stop's lights. They were passing a joint and a brown paper bag amongst them. Loud rap music blared from the back of the SUV, but people passing by on their way to vehicles or the building kept their eyes averted and gave the thug's vehicle a wide berth.

One of them noticed her and tilted his head up in greeting. He threw his hands up in a strange, complicated gesture that resembled pitchforks pointed up to the sky.

He clicked his tongue. "Come on over here shawty. I want to talk to you."

"No thanks," said the woman, nervously. "We're just going to dinner."

The guy elbowed one of his friends and made his way over, his friends trailing behind with odd smiles on their faces. Emily's shoulders tensed. The woman she was with clutched her purse to her chest, eyes narrowed, as the guys moved to intercept them in the middle of the parking lot. The guys started crowding in.

The guy who had nodded at Emily sucked at his teeth. "Nah, lil' mama. I got something you can eat. Fill you both right up. Let me get your number."

"She's a minor, and we don't want trouble." said the woman.

The guy looked over. "Don't worry, lil' mama. It's for my young homie. I want to show him how it's done."

Emily cleared her throat as she stepped between the woman and the guys.

The woman placed a hand on Emily's shoulder. "Emily, dear. We can just get snacks at the next exit."

Emily glanced sidelong at the woman, noting the hand securely clutching her purse and the dangerous gleam in her eye.

"I appreciate what you're trying to do, ma'am. But if it's not me, it'll be some other poor girl who doesn't know how to defend herself."

The woman reluctantly removed her hand.

"I don't have a phone," Emily said with a smile. "Sorry. Move please."

"Aw, that's too bad," he said, reaching into his pocket. He pulled out a phone. "Want one?"

"Not really. I'm not interested."

He nodded and replaced the phone in his pocket. "A'ight, cool. So, lil' mama, what that mouth do?"

Emily kept her face impassive. "Considering this conversation, it's most likely going to hurt your feelings."

A flicker of anger crossed his brow, but he kept an aloof, confident smile. He laughed as one of his friends slapped him on the back with a jibe.

"No need to be shy," he said.

Emily smiled to herself as she gathered her red hair into a ponytail, wrapping an elastic band around it. The signs were clear to her. And, though she'd been kicked out of the Nomad program, these poor guys were woefully unprepared for what she could do to them. The five young men who stood between her and the diner were annoying, and she was tired and hungry.

"Look," said Emily. "You've said a lot of things that you're going to regret, unless you get out of our way."

"Oh, I see," said the guy with a chuckle, one of his trailing friends smacking another guy's shoulder. "You just want us to buy you dinner first, right?"

Emily's smile faded a bit. They still weren't getting the hint. "It would have been better than all the other crap you just said."

The guys were laughing again. "Ah, fo' sho? Shi-, you shoulda said so."

"I did." She shifted. "You just won't stop talking and get out of my way. Now, leave us alone before I have to hurt you."

"You gonna show me some of your moves?" the guy laughed as he reached out confidently, hand open as if to touch her face.

Emily snatched his wrist and twisted it sharply. She felt the bones break, as the guy's eyes changed from smoldering confidence to pain and anger. He grunted and swung his other hand. Emily ducked the blow and slammed an elbow into his gut. As he doubled over, she wrapped her arm around his neck in an awkward headlock.

Big as he was, he'd probably still be able to lift her with only one good arm, so she had to maintain an iron grip on his throat. When he tried to move, she squeezed his throat just enough to catch his attention. He stopped struggling, putting his hands up as much as he could in the circumstance. She didn't let go.

The woman had moved. Judging from the angle, and the way her hand had slipped into the purse, Emily approved. That would be a good firing angle for a pistol. She'd minimize accidentally hitting anyone in the nearby diner. Emily pondered for a moment why the woman had taken so long to get into an advantageous position but settled on the thought that maybe, just maybe, this woman was giving her a chance to resolve the issue herself.

A strange feeling of gratitude washed over Emily. She wasn't being usurped by yet another person playing the hero in her life. Between Nikifor and her brother, she lost her spot on the Nomads. More than likely because those two had made her look too reliant on outside help. They meant well, she was sure, but her current situation was the cost of their interference.

"Here's the thing," she said slowly, "I don't care how strong or dangerous you think you are. If the five of you don't leave us alone, some of you won't go home tonight."

One of the other guys pulled a knife. Another reached for a gun in his waistband. Emily sighed as she forcibly turned the thug in her grip around and pulled the revolver from its spot near the small of her back. She had kept it for special occasions, and this was starting to count. She smiled again as she placed the barrel against the guy's temple. She felt him tremble in her sure grip.

"You boys are a special kind of stupid, aren't you?" she asked, never taking her gaze off the group in front of her.

It's like a whole damn gaggle of Antoines.

The thugs hesitated. She didn't blame them. They were finally starting to understand how much control they really had in this situation. That was to say, none at all.

"If you don't move, I don't get to eat," she said, her finger curling around the trigger in a deliberate motion, making sure they could see it.

"Emily!" hissed the woman. "Can we please not do this? They're not worth the paperwork."

Emily ignored her. "If I kill you, I still don't get to eat. Best-case scenario is you five leave us the hell alone, and I go eat a burger with this lovely lady. Please, for the love of all that is holy, don't make this the worst-case scenario. I'm not sure this poor woman would be able to stomach what I'll do to you boys for getting between me and a meal."

The guy in her grip choked out a reply. "A'ight, a'ight. We'll leave you alone."

She raised an eyebrow, and the others put their weapons away. She removed her grip on the guy and dropped her other

At least, that was her thought until a young woman with light brown hair stepped out of the back door, wearing body armor, with a rifle slung across her chest. She looked oddly familiar to Emily, albeit hard to place. People stared from their booths as three other helmeted soldiers disembarked the vehicle. They turned toward the building.

"Don't call me crazy," said Emily, "but I get the feeling I may need that gun back."

They raised rifles. Snap, snap, snap.

Emily scrambled out of the chair, as screams pierced the air and bullets slammed through the diner's window and drowned out the sound of the suppressed shots. The woman she'd been traveling with slumped without a sound, her face frozen in an expression of confusion and a trail of blood dripping from her temple into her plate. The woman's purse lay on its side on the counter, a portion of the strap visible behind her body.

Another shot crashed through the soda glass where Emily had just been. Bullets snapped into the bar and stools as Emily lurched to find some cover. She chanced a look. The armored young woman shifted her aim immediately. Emily ducked back behind the bar. Bullets chewed through the wood behind her.

I can't reach my gun. Fighting them without it falls into the bad ideas category. She needed to move. Get out before they could surround her. It had to be her they were after. People didn't just go around in body armor shooting up diners for no reason. *Not even in my novels.* But at least they'd made one tactical error she hoped was actually a mistake.

Emily moved quickly around the bar. The waitress crouched on the floor with her head covered. Good instinct. Emily grabbed a glass from the rack beside her and hurled it. As bullets struck the rapidly moving glass, she ripped a heavy skillet from the griddle and slung it at the side window. She ran the other direction and jumped through an open door frame to the Employee area as it bounced off the glass.

"What the hell?" She hissed. "That should have gone straight through! Damn movies!"

Emily surged through to the back door and spilled out into the parking lot. She glanced to her right. The brown-haired girl stood there, her face impassive as she shouldered the rifle and squeezed the trigger again. Emily bolted toward the dumpster. There was only so far she could outrun bullets with all the empty space around her, but she could possibly make it the few feet to the dumpster. And she sure as hell didn't want to go closer to the gas pumps.

Not that the dumpster would be much better. It could work as marginally slim concealment for a sprint into the woods. None of the crap in there would be thick enough to stop rifle rounds. Emily slipped behind the dumpster as bullets tore into it. She dropped to the pavement and covered her head, trying to decide her next move under the barrage of suppressed snaps and the zips of flying metal. It was a miracle nothing hit her, considering. She needed to keep moving.

No, you need to get your gun and shoot back.

Emily considered her options as she crawled towards a nearby stand of trees. She could circle back around to the diner as they searched the woods for her. Maybe she'd get lucky, and there wouldn't be a rifle aimed at her face when she approached the other side of the building.

Except.

Sure enough, Emily saw the brown-haired girl through the trees ahead. Emily cursed and dropped to the dirt as the girl fired several shots her way. She rose and sprinted in the other direction, coming around again to the back door of the diner. A helmeted man appeared in the doorway with his rifle aimed at her chest.

Emily ran full speed, dipping low to tackle him. The man let out a pained grunt as he was pushed into the back office area of the diner. When they hit the floor, Emily snatched the knife from its holster on his chest and plunged it into his throat, ignoring the wet squelch as blood flowed around the blade. She reached for his rifle, but there was a noise behind her. Emily rolled to the side. Suppressed bullets hit the dead man a moment later.

It was getting harder to breathe. The waitress lay there, face down in a pool of blood. Without hesitation, Emily hopped over the bar counter. Bodies lay everywhere, the linoleum covered in a bloody spray. She shook her head to focus on the current fight. *I can feel bad after I survive.*

Without looking, she snatched the woman's purse and grabbed the guns. She thanked the woman silently as she pulled an extra magazine for the Glock pistol. Model 19C. Emily would have to be careful. Counting her Vindicator, which would translate to thirty-six shots at most. And with three targets actively hunting her, it didn't feel like enough ammunition.

Emily took a few moments to catch her breath as she slipped the Vindicator back into the waistband holster, keeping the Glock in hand. A movement caught her eye, and she raised the Glock instinctively, stopping short as a man raised pudgy hands and gestured at her.

"Emily, thank God," said the man. "Come with me. We've got to get you out of here."

Emily didn't know who this man was, but he wasn't trying to shoot her. She bolted, hitting the door at a sprint. The man ducked as shots zipped by. Emily turned and shot back; the Glock's sound thunderous in the night air. The orange glow of the muzzle flash was too bright. Too disorienting. The man she shot at turned the corner to shoot, and she fired three more rounds.

He staggered a moment, mechanically ignoring it to lean his rifle around the corner. As he sighted in, Emily took another shot, the bullet striking the man's ballistic helmet. His shot went wild. She ran, following the pudgy man to a large black sedan parked near a pump.

They ripped the doors open and got in. The car was already running. *That's strange,* Emily thought. The pudgy man put the car in reverse and drove over the curb to get back onto the highway. Emily's head struck the ceiling lightly, and she glared at him as she rubbed the spot. Shifting gears, he gunned the engine, the car picking up speed with a deep roar.

"Keep your head down; we'll lose them in a few miles."

Emily pressed the button to roll her window down. "Forgive me if I don't believe you. These people just shot up a diner in the middle of the night. Why would they stop now?"

She leaned out just as the headlights of the black SUV turned from the parking lot to point at them. The SUV disappeared for a few moments behind a low rise on the highway. The glow of the SUV's headlights brightened the horizon just before they crested the hill.

The brown-haired girl's head and shoulders emerged through the sunroof of the SUV, and she braced her rifle on the roof. She fired several shots, forcing Emily to duck down.

"As long as they're using subsonic ammunition, we'll be fine if we're in the car. The car is armored," said the pudgy man.

She leaned out as the firing stopped. Emily hoped the lull in gunfire was because the brown-haired girl was changing magazines. She could barely make out the form of another shooter leaning out the side window, firing with somewhat less accuracy at Emily. Emily fired the Glock, aiming low. She couldn't tell if she'd hit anything with the first few shots.

The pudgy man tugged at the back of her shirt. "Stay in the damn car. I'm trying to keep you alive, in case you hadn't noticed."

She glared at him, her finger resting on the pistol's trigger guard. She snarled, "Touch me again, and you won't live long enough to worry."

Pudgy chuckled. "You're tough, but you're not that scary, kiddo."

She fired a few more shots. "And you're not a great getaway driver. Care to slow down and get control of this thing?"

"You want to get shot? Because that's how you get shot."

Emily hissed. "I can't hit a thing with you swerving everywhere. Get me an angle and I can end this."

Emily's gut dropped as the car rapidly decelerated. A few seconds later, the SUV's grill made contact, jostling them.

"Better, Mom?" said the pudgy man.

"How are you driving worse at a slower speed?"

Emily leaned out, aimed, and pulled the trigger several times. The SUV started to swerve. Raising the barrel, she took shots through the windshield. One lucky shot must have hit the driver. The SUV skittered off the shoulder, flipping in the moonlight and rolling across the low grass with several deep crunches.

Emily collapsed back in her seat and checked the Glock. Chamber empty, slide locked. She sent a silent word of thanks to the dead woman for the weapon that had saved her life. So much death. And for what? Why could Emily be so important that people were willing to shoot innocents just to kill her?

She felt heat behind her eyes but blinked back the regret she felt. How could she have done anything differently? It didn't make sense to blame herself for the deaths, but somehow, she still felt responsible. The dead woman. Emily had ignored her name. Would there be anyone left to grieve for her? Surely, there would. Surely such a kindhearted woman had friends.

Emily glanced at the pudgy man, wondering who he was, and whether he was involved with the woman. Must have been, considering how close he'd been when the shooting started.

She loaded the fresh magazine into the gun and pocketed everything. Then, she slumped in the seat. All her belongings had been in the woman's car, aside from the gun. No book, no nothing.

If she had one fully realized regret, it was that she'd been in the middle of a chapter when they'd stopped. She allowed the image of a dark-haired girl wearing a white t-shirt with a panther on it, to enter her mind. In spite of herself, Emily wished she had friends like Jade, the protagonist. Someone excited to see her at lunch. A road trip with friends.

The adrenaline of the fight drained from her body. Her eyes closed as the pudgy man drove on into the night. At some point, a vague sensation of something cold crossed her wrists with a soft click.

5 Unveiled Nightmare

Steven answered Abaroa's call. He couldn't make out any of the words. They were too garbled. He looked at the phone. There was no reception icon. Instead, it displayed the notification "Searching for network…"

He sighed. The sounds of the school filtered back in: crashing furniture and shattering glass. The cries of scared students and the roars of monsters battled for priority.

Glancing at the huddled mass of students in the corner of the room, he fought an urge to shout at them. They needed to get moving. Lives depended on Steven's ability to keep going, despite the fear gripping his heart like a vice. He held his free hand out to Grace. She took it, helping to pull Mirena out from under the desk.

"Did you drive today?" he asked.

Grace tilted her head. "I did. But my car is in student parking. We'd have to go through the building to get there."

Steven scratched at his head. He eliminated going through the building as an option. "Not necessarily. We can go around the back of the building. There's a fence separating the faculty and student parking lots. I don't think they'll worry about me popping the gate lock today."

Mirena rubbed at her eyes. "Ay Dios Mio, nene! And if there's more of them out there?"

"Point is, we're not staying here," he said. "I can get you there, but you have to trust me."

"Trust you?" demanded Mirena, face scrunched. "You brought a gun to school, pendejo. I don't have to trust anything you say."

He narrowed his eyes. "Fine, then. Don't trust me. But you don't have a choice. I'm your only chance to get out of here alive, and I'm not leaving you to die. Let's go."

As he turned away, Grace tugged at his arm. The fear on her face overrode the stern set of his gaze.

Grace kept her voice firm. "We're scared. Be nice."

Steven hung his head, "I'll try. But we need to get moving. If we don't get ahead of this, we won't make it."

Grace nodded, fixing her eyes resolutely on his. He wondered at her resolve. She fought against the fear. Every shuddered breath urged him to move, to act. He squeezed her hand, forcing a smile.

He let go and turned to the open door, walking until he could peer around at the hallway. The empty corridor took on an eeriness, blood smears and shoe prints jumbled in every direction. On the other hand, they were a few feet from the exit to the faculty parking lot. If he could get them to Grace's car, it might be enough.

Steven took the first few steps into the hallway. People crowded around behind him, some attempting to peek into the hallway. Grace, Mirena, and the knot of survivors. Their concerned whispers were too loud.

He turned back to gesture for silence as they all moved. The group of survivors shoved past Steven and the girls to the side door of the school. He kept his gun low, but ready to aim down the hallway at a moment's notice. He walked in the opposite direction of the fleeing group to a nearby door that led to the faculty parking area, glancing back over his shoulder from time to time as they approached the exit.

Steven fought to open the outer door. A body lay propped against it. He switched hands on the gun long enough to shove more of his weight into the door. He stumbled out as the door caught, dragging the body a few inches. He caught himself from tripping by holding onto the door.

He shook his head. Smoke swirled in the air. Evidence of a nearby fire stung his eyes and throat. Tires squealed and metal crunched somewhere close. The afternoon sky held a strange glow. Steven led them out of the corridor to an outdoor passage.

The walls to either side held broken windows. At the end of the passage was a sidewalk. To the right, it would lead north, toward the mall. Left would lead around the building to student parking. He approached the corner with trepidation, sweeping the open space before him with the Glock.

What the hell could be on fire?

Most of the cars in the faculty lot looked untouched. It suddenly seemed like a hell of a lot of open space between the building and the fence to the student parking area. Snarls and growls from prowling creatures floated in the wind, echoing off buildings. He made out the indistinct forms of three monsters in the student parking lot.

Grace pressed into his back with a whimper. She trembled, despite her calm exterior. He thanked whatever deity might be listening for Grace and Mirena staying with him.

"Stay low. I don't want to try covering that much distance in the open like this. Not without a lot more bullets, at least."

Grace looked around, pointing across to the gate. "Why not? That way looks clear."

She doesn't see the monsters in the lot yet. Hopefully, they'll move on before we get there.

"Three monsters in student parking that'll be able to overtake us if we're not careful enough. Follow me," he said, face pinched.

The three crouch-walked around the brick facade, hugging the wall until they came around to a second passage. Just beyond the external stairwell to the library, two double doors on the ground floor standing sentry, a dark spatter obscuring one of the door's built-in windows. A figure emerged from the double doors, catching his eye.

Something glinted in the figure's hand. Steven raised the Glock in reflex and pushed Grace and Mirena back toward the corner of the building. He rounded the staircase to face the potential threat.

The old teacher swiped sweaty silver hair from his face, taking a long look at the gun pointed his way. Harper's torn black shirt showed fresh blood, and more stained his belt buckle.

Dr. Harper smiled nervously. "Mr. Fuller, I presume."

"Wait, I thought..." Steven trailed off. Dr. Harper's voice was too calm. Every classroom Steven remembered passing held a mutated teacher, a monster. The school employed at least eighty teachers. What were the chances only one escaped the mutation? What the hell even caused it? There were too many questions without answers.

"Looks like you have a plan, as always." Harper fidgeted with the pistol in his hand.

Steven hesitated before responding. "Something like that."

Harper scoffed, his eyes soft with something akin to defeat. "No, boy. You're adjusting your plan based on what you see ahead of you. I know the look. I'm the reason you have it."

"Are you alright, sir?" said Steven.

Harper raised an eyebrow. "Yes, Mr. Fuller. I'm certainly fine. Liberated, if you will. Richards can test all he wants to, now."

Steven narrowed his eyes. "What the hell are you talking about? Who is Richards?"

Harper's eyes went wild. "No, Steven. You can't have my secrets. No one can have them ever again."

Harper's hand flicked out, and he squeezed the trigger of the compact pistol. The skin on Steven's cheek flared in pain as he returned fire. He pressed the trigger twice in rapid succession. Two bullets struck Harper in the center of his chest. The holes were less than a centimeter apart. The man's triumphant expression turned sour and fearful as his gun hand dropped. He put his other hand over the wound, staring at it in wonderment.

"You filthy creature," he wheezed, dropping to his knees. "Who knew you would be my salvation?"

Nearby roars startled Steven back into motion. He stepped forward and kicked Harper's dropped pistol away from the man's failing body. Harper's wide eyes moved wildly, unfocused. He lay there, trembling in a growing crimson ring.

Steven turned back and motioned for Grace and Mirena to head to the stairs.

"Is he dead?" asked Grace.

Steven grimaced. "Not yet, but it won't be long now."

Mirena hesitated at the corner, flinching back from him. "You're insane. You just shot a teacher!"

He pointed at the fresh cut on his cheek. "If it makes you feel any better, he shot at me first."

"Why would that make me feel better?"

"We don't have time for this, Mirena!" Steven hissed. He regretted the outburst as she flinched again, eyes wide and glistening.

He sighed and spoke softer. "I'm sorry. I know you're scared. I am, too. I'll die to keep you safe, but I'd rather only face that when it becomes necessary. Now, let's go. Up the stairs to the library. We can get to the roof from there."

He followed as they ascended, aiming his gun down the stairs. He bumped into Grace. She was gazing at the body down below. Harper had stopped trembling, his still body staring sightlessly into the sky above.

He spoke softly. "I know this is hard to deal with. Try not to think about it until we're safe on the roof."

"Why the roof?" said Mirena. "I thought we were going to the parking lot."

"We are," said Steven. "But we need a safer way to get there."

They reached the top just as a misshapen face came around the corner of the building, the monster digging its claws into the nearby brick. Another lurched around after the first, snapping its jaws with a snarl. Steven urged Grace and Mirena into the door to the library.

In an overlooked corner of the silent library, Steven located the roof access door.

Thankfully, the wooden door itself would be easy enough to break. The problem would be the steel frame holding the locking mechanism. He examined the hinges. It was a pull door, because of course he couldn't catch a break.

He tried the handle. The latch didn't move with it. Steven took a breath, swallowing the frustration building in his body. A dull thud sounded from the external stairway door. No time to be safe about it. Steven stepped back and took aim at the handle.

"Take cover," he said.

As the girls moved, the door in front of him clicked and opened. A young woman wearing an eye patch, with pale skin, and pixie-cut black hair stood in front of him. She smiled at his confused expression and ran a hand through a silver highlight.

Despite her intense face and a single eye the color of a rain cloud, Nyura Petrowycz batted her long eyelashes and smiled playfully. "Hiya, Steven. Fancy seeing you and your girlfriends here. What a player."

Letting out an unintentional groan, Steven glared at her. "Nyura, please. Not now."

Nyura turned away from the door with a huff, climbing the ladder to a hatch above. Steven let Grace and Mirena go before him, closing the door behind himself with a soft click, letting the automatic lock engage. Moments later, a loud burst of noise like splitting kindling made his skin prickle. Snarls and growling from the room beyond the door grew louder, more frantic. The sounds of falling shelves and books being torn apart echoed through the tiny space. He wondered momentarily if the monsters were following scents or sounds. He decided it didn't matter.

Steven double-checked and pocketed the Glock. He climbed the steel ladder as quietly as his boots would allow, touching only toe-tips to the rungs. He emerged into the afternoon sunlight. Grace and Mirena held hands, standing just to the side of the hatch. The group before him, while welcome, was a startling sight. Nyura, Pattie, Brice, and Kathryn.

He noticed Ladeen, sitting huddled to one side of an air conditioning unit, tended to by a well-bandaged Curtis. The last time he'd seen her was in the office the day before. She looked frightened now, and nursed a couple of new scrapes, but looked relatively okay.

"Is this it?" Steven whispered.

Curtis sneered. "What do you think?"

Kathryn hugged herself, eyes brimming with tears. "We tried. No one would follow me."

"What about..." he hesitated, but shook his head of the stupid protocols holding him back. "What about the others from the arsenal? Karl, and Ernest?"

Curtis glared at Steven. Ladeen placed a hand on the man's cheek to turn his attention back, but Curtis showed more interest in staring daggers. Ladeen shoved him away and hugged herself. Curtis's eyes went wide, and he tried putting a hand on hers. She turned away from him, staring at the roof. He got to his feet and turned toward Steven, eyes narrowed.

"This is what I was talking about before," Curtis growled. "Good for you, you convinced two chicks to follow you to the roof in that hell. Sorry, we weren't good enough."

Brice shook his head. "Back off, man. That's not what Steven was getting at, and you know it."

Curtis mumbled something and turned to glare out across the roof.

Nyura closed the roof hatch and sat on it, crossing her skirted legs and shifting her startling gray eye between Curtis and Steven. She smiled deviously.

"You know, he hasn't shut up about it," she said.

Steven snorted, "Let me guess, I don't fight fair?"

Nyura said, "Right. Too bad for him, we all know you've trained with the Nomads." She laughed, gesturing. "Well, I guess not those three. Different after-school activities for them. I must say, I am surprised you left him breathing, considering what you looked like after your 'spar' yesterday."

"Has anybody gotten through to Abaroa or anyone else at home?" Steven pulled his phone, checking again for a signal.

"Of course not." She shook her head. "Cell towers are jammed, and nobody's going to the office in this mess to use the landline."

Steven raised an eyebrow. "Jammed? Are you sure?"

"Like toast," she said, pulling her cell phone for evidence. "Searching for a network. In the middle of a city, even a backwater like this one. That's a sure sign to me."

Curtis stalked over. "If it isn't the prodigal chosen one. Leave it to the weirdo to survive hell on earth."

Crossing his arms and gazing around the roof, Steven narrowed his eyes and sighed. "We have bigger problems right now than what's going on between us. Let it go for now."

Curtis returned his glare. "Shut up! We've got standing orders from Abaroa. He's traced something back to your homeroom teacher, Dr. Harper. We need to capture Harper and take him back to base."

Shrugging, Steven stared at him blankly. "That's going to be a problem. Harper's dead."

Mouth agape, Curtis clenched his fists. "You've got to be joking. Please tell me you're not serious."

Steven pointed at the stinging cut on his cheek. "He pulled a gun and fired. So, I shot back. Either way, unless you want to go to the parking lot and collect the body, he's not coming with us."

Nyura looked around. "So, what do we do then?"

Taking in the gathering on the roof, Steven shrugged. "I don't know about you six, but I'm getting Grace and Mirena to safety."

"I wonder if you can take me straight on." Curtis sneered, feinting at Steven. "Abandoning the mission like a coward. I mean, it's like you've got two brain cells fighting over being in third place."

Steven waited, silent and watchful. Curtis bounced on his feet, breathing quicker. He threw a fast jab. Steven grabbed the other young man's arm and tripped him. Before Curtis could react to the pain, Steven pressed a boot down, pinning Curtis to the roof by his throat.

Steven said, "I don't know why you've never liked me, and I don't care. You want to be stupid and get yourself killed, be my guest. But I refuse to be targeted by those things because you won't stop being petty for once in your life."

Nyura cleared her throat and said, "So, let me rephrase this. What's the plan, boss?"

The rest of the group gathered around. Steven took his boot off of Curtis.

"Why are you asking me?" Steven stepped back, leaving Curtis to be disgusted by his humiliation.

Grinning, Nyura put her hands on her hips and turned to Grace. "You like this guy? He's dense as a bagel!"

The others shared a nervous laugh, making Nyura smile wider.

Brice grinned. "Where, exactly, do you get your bagels?"

"The Arsenal commissary. Why? You got a better place to pick up bagels?"

"Um, yeah!" he said, gesturing wildly. "The bread store on Fifth! Y'all know we're allowed to leave the base every once in a while, right?"

They were attempting to break the tension, he supposed. But he couldn't think of a way to get them all out. Not unless there were at least two vehicles between them.

"Either way," said Nyura, turning back to Steven. "You've got your head on straight, and we need a plan. You got top marks on the last tactical assessment. Like it or not, I'm following you. I just need to know how close to follow."

"As of the moment," Steven looked pointedly at Nyura, "my plan hasn't changed. I need to get these two to Grace's parents. I don't think there'll be enough room in her car for everyone here, though."

"And after they're safe?" she asked, playing with a zipper on her hip pouch.

Steven ran his fingers through his hair. "I'd like to fix one problem at a time if you don't mind."

Mirena pointed at Nyura. "I've always wanted to ask. What's with the eyepatch?"

"Oh, this?" Nyura smiled, framing her face with her hands. "Well, one day, I was trying to seduce Pattie and walked face-first into a tree branch. Hurt like hell, but now I know what keeping an eye out really means."

Pattie rolled her eyes as Mirena's went wide.

"Seriously?" Steven grinned. "You told me you were socializing a crow, and it didn't like the gift you gave it."

Nyura put a finger to her lips. "Did I? Ah, well...what really happened was, I was fishing with my dad, and he caught my face. Turns out trout love eyeballs."

Steven smiled to himself.

Grace put a hand on his elbow. "It's a long way home, Steven. What happens if you don't make it?"

Steven forced a smile. "Strip what you need from my body and keep fighting."

He turned back to the gathering, "Fine. Listen closely. As of the moment, this is about survival, first and foremost. Everything else you think might be an objective is secondary."

Nyura nodded, reaching behind where she'd been sitting for a messenger bag. She pulled out a notebook and a pen and handed them to Kathryn. Kathryn began sketching.

"Where does Grace live?" asked Kathryn.

Grace gave her address and Nyura nodded slowly.

Kathryn said, "First problem, the streets are going to be congested with stopped cars. When I checked a few minutes ago, there were at least three on fire at the nearest intersection. Not to mention the monsters in the parking lot. Second problem, her street's quite a ways, but there's an Arsenal safehouse in the commercial district between here and there. From here to her house, we're looking at five miles of extremely hostile territory. Two from here to the safehouse."

Kathryn handed the notebook to Steven. She'd drawn an approximate map of the area and the route.

Steven looked over the map. "You're sure about this safe house?"

Nyura rolled her eye, giving Steven a half-smile. "Of course she is. I told her about it. There's plenty of extra equipment there. Weapons, gear, food, and vehicles."

Steven nodded as a plan began to solidify. "How'd you get permission to go there?"

She smiled a disarming smile. "Abaroa had me double-check the medical stocks last time I..." she trailed off, with a sidelong glance at Pattie. "Last time I got in trouble. You're not the only troublemaker. Just the most paranoid."

Pattie walked over and put out her hand. Steven handed Pattie his gun, and she looked it over. She cleared it, pulling the magazine and ejecting the chambered round.

"Model 26. Cool. Fifteen round mag, plus one, and it's down by two rounds. Who'd you kill to get this?"

She put it all back together with an appreciative nod.

Steven fought another shrug. He became keenly aware how much he'd done that in the last hour alone. Face impassive, he said, "I suspect I filled out the same requisition forms you did for extended practice."

Faking a pout, she shrugged. "You got me. I'm using a 43, though."

His brow creased in disbelief. "Seriously? That's only six shots."

She handed the gun back, grinning. "Well, shot placement counts for something. Don't need high capacity when you hit every target. Also, it left room for extra mags."

"Fair enough," Steven said, then laid out the plan. He pointed at Curtis who, for his part, was still sulking nearby. "For your own sake, if no one else's. Once we get moving, don't do anything stupid."

Curtis glared. "Like what? Very little would be stupider than following you."

"You're free to go your own way," said Steven with a dismissive hand wave.

Curtis practically spat at Steven. "What is it with you? Do you think you're better than the rest of us? It's so freaking infuriating, I just want to punch your face in."

Putting a palm to his own forehead, Steven's face scrunched. "Is that what it's all about? That's why you've been picking fights with me? I don't see how I'm the one thinking that way."

"See it from our angle," said Curtis. "You're like the golden child, getting special training with the Nomads. Weapons requisition permission? Admit it, you're Abaroa's favorite."

Steven raised an eyebrow. "Clearly, Patti has the same permissions. You probably could have, too, if you weren't an ass." How could he explain training with the Nomads as a punishment? *Not for my growth. That training was designed to break me completely.* He wondered--not for the first time--how close he was to being broken.

"That's your angle alone. We've all been in the darkness, Curtis. Everyone in this program has experienced some of the worst traumas this life can dish out. Don't let my attempts to survive be what crushes you. You're better than that. Otherwise, you wouldn't still be here. And we've already lost enough people."

Curtis looked pensive. His entire body drooped; lips held tightly together. Finally, he sighed. "So, what do I do?"

Steven said, "The only way to fly is to take a leap of faith and build your wings on the way down."

Ladeen scoffed. "That's what you're going with? You're quoting the posters in Hogan's office now?"

Steven chuckled. "Maybe he's had more of an effect than I give him credit for."

They all shared a nervous laugh. Curtis extended a hand, which Steven accepted, and they shook.

Not friends. Not quite. But at least we're not enemies at the moment. Tentative allies, perhaps.

They crept along the roof in a loose line, Steven leading the group with Pattie working rear security. Steven swept his eyes across the rooftop as they went, scanning for movement. They reached the other end without incident and found a locked roof hatch over the main office.

The roof extended further to their right and skirted the parking lot. A pair of sky bridges connected an addition to the building, leading to the gym and sports field parking lot. A magnolia tree's branches peeked from the other side of the farthest sky bridge.

Steven smiled. "Who here likes climbing trees?" He chuckled at the collective groan from his companions.

"Don't worry," he said, clearing the Glock and pocketing it. "I can go first. If anything kills me, go a different way."

Nyura stared at him pointedly with a raised eyebrow. Her expression seemed to say, "Really?"

As they approached the tree, Steven assessed the climb.

"Good news," he said. "There's only a short drop from the lowest branches to the ground."

Pattie snorted. "How the hell is that the good news?"

He shrugged. "It's quieter than shooting our way through the building to the ground floor."

Curtis glared. "And if they hear us and come looking?"

"Right now, it looks like they're still uncoordinated." Steven squatted at the edge of the sky bridge, then sat, dangling his legs over the edge. "If we're quick, we've got mobility on our side. Use what's around you and run like hell. Leave fighting back to me and Pattie."

Pattie cleared her throat.

"My bad," said Steven, shaking his head with a suppressed laugh. "Leave the fighting to Pattie and me."

"Much better," Pattie said, grabbing a branch. "Also, you're trash at climbing, and I don't want to be stuck up here waiting to see if you mess up."

She stepped over onto the tree and descended in deliberate motions, a clear attempt to minimize making noise.

Mirena put a hand to her head. "Que mierda! I can't do that."

Steven's eyes widened as Grace slapped Mirena's arm, eliciting a short, quiet yelp from the other girl.

Mirena looked sheepish. "Sorry. It slipped. I'm stressed out."

Grace hugged her. "I get it. But chill out. We're going to make it."

"How do you know?" Mirena's eyes glistened, red and puffy. Her lips quivered with every breath.

Nyura placed a gentle hand on Mirena's shoulder. Nyura ran her other hand through one of the silver highlights of her hair, her face beaming with a sudden smile.

"You've made a mistake, and picked up some really badass friends," said Nyura with a wink. She moved quickly to descend the tree behind Pattie.

One by one, they climbed down the tree. Steven and Curtis were the last to descend.

"Alright, everybody. Same game plan as before. Stay low, stay quiet. Watch our backs, Pattie." Steven readied his weapon and took his position at the head of the group.

They moved as swiftly as they dared, rounding the west side of the building. To their right, Steven made out a pair of monsters through the chain-link parking lot fence, fighting viciously over a body. He forced himself to ignore the sight, turning left to pass through the narrow gap between the building and an old gymnasium.

For a moment, he recalled his conversation with Grace. After commissioning the new gym, the school converted the old one into an auto shop, providing additional space for students on a trade path. Steven shook his head and silently cursed. He needed to focus.

A small section of additional parking lay before him. Beyond the tarmac, the former softball field stretched until it met the road beyond. They would be exposed for an uncomfortable amount of time. The inevitability of the path before Steven loomed, threatening to destroy his resolve.

A deep, throaty growl from ahead caught his attention. He couldn't see the monster who issued it, but he knew it would be close enough to be a threat. They couldn't just stand there. They needed to get moving. Of all times to freeze, this couldn't be one.

His father's voice spoke in his head. "When you're fighting, speed is life. When it goes down, don't go slow unless you wanna die."

Steven narrowed his eyes and took a step.

Hell of a pep talk for a seven-year-old, huh, Dad?

The last time he hesitated, his father paid the price. The last time, Steven himself clung to life only because that was what he knew his father expected. Another step. Steven picked up speed, gathering distance between himself and the group. Breaking his own rule. Breaking the formation. They would need time and space to get around the fight. Precious seconds would be the only thing standing between this group of survivors and certain death. The growl grew louder. The monster knew they were there.

It barreled around the gymnasium. It took long strides across the field like a great beast, with misshapen, previously human features. A mask of blood and teeth. Its claws dug into the dirt, propelling it in an unerring charge, straight at Steven. He stopped, leaned into his stance and centered his sights on a point ahead of the monster. He pulled in a deep breath, releasing it slowly. By the end of the exhale, the monster had bounded over half the distance to him.

Damn, but they can run. Fifty meters in ten seconds is nothing to sneeze at.

Steven held his breath at the exhale a few seconds more until the monster came just outside a good dueling distance. Steven ignored the feelings of having known this person. The dark hair was matted with dried blood. The formerly stern, but pretty face. He would remember Coach Gladys Jonston as one of the few teachers who seemed to give a damn about how he felt on a regular basis.

Steven pulled the trigger, and the former coach's knee buckled. She rolled momentarily, clawing at the dirt ahead with inhuman vigor. He centered the gun, firing a second shot into her head. It snapped up, then she fell limp to the grass. Roars echoed off the buildings behind them.

He shouted, "No more low and slow. Maybe we can break their line of sight in the woods behind the church across the street. Get moving!"

Pattie chimed at him, "How about let's aim for the head first next time, yeah?"

Steven smiled. "I'll save the trick shots for you. Make sure the others get across to the church."

He glanced behind the group. Several monsters converged on them. Moving fast. Not as fast as the coach, but fast enough.

Apparently, some correlation existed between former fitness levels and the monsters' current abilities. Steven filed away the observation to ruminate on later. As the others ran ahead, he counted. Four from the student parking lot. Two from the other side of the new gym. Too many to face head-on.

The four from the parking lot had to bunch up to pass through the gap between the buildings. Steven smiled, firing twice. The lead monster's leg gave out, and the other three stumbled over it in their haste. The pile of creatures writhed as they fought amongst each other, trying to be the first to get up.

The other two were too spread out at the moment. Steven decided not to chance a shot and ran behind the group. He could tell from their speed he wasn't going to make it behind the church before they overtook him. But maybe he could get them to line up like the other four.

As he drew closer to the group, someone stumbled and fell. Mirena cursed, holding her knee. Steven reached down and yanked her to her feet. She cried out.

"I know it hurts," he said quickly, softly. "Push through it. You have to keep going."

Brice jogged back. "I've got her. Keep us safe, Rambo."

"Roger that, I've got your six." Steven smiled grimly.

Brice helped Mirena into a saddleback carry, arms wrapped around his neck. He turned and kept moving. Unfortunately, he was slower now. The rest of the group slowed as well.

I made the wrong call. Dammit! We're going to die because I made the wrong call.

Eight out of sixteen shots gone. Six targets he could see, running to overtake the group in less than thirty seconds. The city of Blue Rock falling into shambles around him. He pulled the pistol in close, switching his stance. Almost hugging the gun in his grip. Pattie appeared next to him, aiming her pistol at one of the two from the right. She fired, hitting it in the face. It dropped.

She drew in another breath. "The others are almost across. I've got the two on the right." The creature ahead moved erratically, and her second shot missed.

Steven strode with smooth purpose as close as he dared and fired his first shot less than ten yards away. He hit the monster in the head, dropping it as he spun away from its charge. He shot the next one through the eye, ignoring his nausea as its head split open.

Steven remembered seeing death before. The death surrounding him was as familiar as greeting an old friend. Hearing Pattie's shot, and a yelp of pain, something inside him broke. Mirena's math teacher. Dr. Harper. Coach Jonston. Now, these six. His actions were taking lives. He pulled the trigger, striking the third of four in the throat. It gurgled as it collapsed, a claw slicing Steven's shoulder.

As Steven stumbled from the searing pain of the gash on his arm, the final monster rushed in with a powerful strike. Its head snapped to the side, a red splash from its temple. Steven glanced over at Pattie. Her dark eyes were thoughtful on her pale face, asking a question. He didn't want to think about the answer yet.

I don't have time to worry about myself. Granted, who knows if I'll ever be okay?

Pattie grimaced, holding a hand to her side. A patch of dark red discolored her bright yellow t-shirt, ribbons of blood along her hand and leg.

He asked, "How bad is it?"

"Worse than yours," she said, gritting her teeth against the pain. "This is going to be a long-ass two miles."

"We're going to make it." He ignored the stab of pain in his chest from what he felt was a lie. Her face drained of more color with each passing breath. He let her pocket her pistol and wrap an arm around his neck. They trudged through the church parking lot, into the small stand of trees behind it. He breathed a sigh as he caught sight of the group. They were still moving.

Nyura watched their approach, raising a hand in greeting. Her triumphant grin slipped, and her face contorted in shock. She clamped a hand to her mouth, using the other to motion for the others to stop. They waited as Steven helped Pattie and they made their way to the others.

"Your girlfriend's gonna get jealous when she sees us like this." Pattie half-grinned, half-winced. The false bravado must have been for his benefit.

Steven could only guess at how much pain Pattie was in. He'd need to distract her from it somehow.

Steven grunted, Pattie's weight digging into his injured shoulder. "If she's that volatile, I'm better off learning now than later."

"The girl's been cussing at you since I met her a few minutes ago," Pattie giggled.

Steven groaned. *Damn Mirena and her constant attention.*

Pattie slumped against him. Her breathing became too shallow. Too quick. She was going into shock. He needed to keep her talking.

"Pretty sure Grace is trying to claim me, not Mirena. But to be fair," he said, "I technically don't have a girlfriend."

She grinned up at him, smacking her lips as though thirsty. "What the hell's technical about it? You're either with someone or you're not. We're in high school, hot shot. Get with the program. Hell, you could get away with dating them both, you play your cards right."

He forced a chuckle. "You're a right pain in the ass, you know that?"

Pattie croaked a laugh of her own. "Momma always said so. At least I'm pretty, though. Right? You do think I'm pretty, right?"

Steven's forced smile drained away. "All of a sudden, I don't feel qualified for this discussion."

Relief flooded Steven as they caught up to the group. Nyura cursed softly. She directed Steven and together they sat Pattie next to a tree. He hoped they had enough cover with the surrounding foliage.

Pattie's breaths came in ragged gasps. Her face pinched in pain with every inhalation.

Nyura moved with practiced precision, examining the wound. There was a small hole in Pattie's side, under her ribcage. It looked like a stab wound, but too jagged. Nyura pulled a paper-wrapped object from the pouch on her hip and unwrapped it.

"Good thinking," said Steven, recognizing the object. A tampon would plug the hole temporarily, hopefully help stop the bleeding. Granted, as deep as the wound went, it could be a delaying tactic. Steven tried not to call it false hope in his mind, but the shadow of the thought played across his face.

"Yeah," said Nyura with a grimace. "Too bad she's going to hate me for this."

Nyura shoved the tampon into the hole. Pattie grunted through the pain of it. The blood in the wound began engorging the absorbent cotton, blocking the pathway in seconds. Nyura pulled a small knife from the pouch and took off the shirt she'd been wearing. Steven turned away but then realized the girl wore a tank-top undershirt.

She worked quickly, breaking the shirt down into long strips. She wrapped them tightly around Pattie's body, putting additional pressure on the wound. Finally, Nyura pulled a silver cylinder from the pouch. It looked about the size of a tube of lipstick.

She pulled a cap from the cylinder, revealing a hypodermic needle. She shoved the needle into the skin near Pattie's wound, pressing on the rear of the cylinder. Pattie's face flushed with color in moments. She groaned in pain, her fingers digging into the loam beside the tree.

"Holy hell," wheezed Pattie. "You're not kidding. I seriously hate you for saving my life just now."

"Hush now," Nyura said. She placed a gentle kiss on the other girl's forehead. "I did all I could. I stopped the bleeding for now, but you know the hemostatic only last so long. Catch your breath, so we can keep moving to the safehouse. I can do more for you there."

Pattie nodded, leaning her head back against the tree with a pained, but contented smile.

"I made you kiss me," she sang in a languid, staccato tune. "In front of people."

Nyura hissed at her with a grin, kissing her again. "Shut it, Baretto!"

"Yes, ma'am," Pattie giggled, her wound pulsing with the movement of her torso. She wore a crooked smile. She would have looked devious, if not for the scrunch of her forehead.

Steven shuffled from foot to foot, glancing around the small section of woods they were hiding in. Depending on how many monsters escaped the school, this spot couldn't last much longer. He moved to the others, looking them over for obvious injuries. Aside from Mirena's skinned knee, Steven didn't find anything of note.

Curtis sat, still and emotionless, watching the action before him as Ladeen held his hand. Grace sat in the grass; knees held to her chest. Mirena's hands covered her eyes, head tilted down. She trembled; every muscle taut.

Mirena asked, "Are we gonna die? Is she?"

Steven attempted to put a hand on Mirena's shoulder, but she twisted away, batting out at his hand. He dropped the gesture.

"She'll be fine, for now," he said, matter-of-factly. "Nyura's the best field medic we could ask for. If she's not worried, we shouldn't be, either."

Nyura shrugged. "I appreciate your confidence in my abilities. I'll do my best."

"I know you will." Steven smiled. "I trust everyone here will. How soon do you think it'll be before it's safe to move her?"

Nyura looked around. "A few minutes, but she'll need help."

Curtis squeezed Ladeen's hand before releasing it and rising to his feet. "I can carry Pattie, for now, that's the best I've got."

Steven nodded. "Don't shortchange yourself, Curtis."

"Don't you dare," Curtis scoffed, eyes narrowed. "You don't get to preach to me. I watched enough of that fight to really understand the differences between us."

Steven shook his head, taking a sidelong glance at the young man standing in front of him. "What's this, now? I thought we were done with that."

"You're done with it." Curtis shoved an accusatory finger at Steven. "You're like a damn machine. I bet you don't even care when you take lives."

Clenching his fists and jaw, Steven scowled. "What the hell do you want from me? Nobody is coming to save us. And, despite your best efforts, I'm doing my best to keep you alive."

He stopped talking, letting the silence settle into an uncomfortable crescendo. Steven's pulse raced, the blood crashing through his body. He was still too keyed up from fighting the monsters but knew better than to back down. If Curtis wanted to force a fight here, he would get everything he bargained for, and more. Curtis sneered, nostrils flared.

Steven knew the darkness within. He had befriended it many years before. The others in the Special Operations Program thought they knew what he faced. Steven hardened his gaze to match Curtis, then let just a bit more surface. The little boy who became a monster.

Curtis's eyes shifted, and he moved as if to hug himself. When the arm in the sling didn't keep up, Curtis dropped the tension in submission.

"If that's how you feel about me keeping you safe," said Steven, measuring his words. He poked Curtis squarely in the middle of his chest. "Then, so be it. Hate me with every weak ass breath I left in you yesterday and be grateful I don't hold a grudge. I hope the bridge you're burning lights your way."

6 The Scars Beneath

Emily buried her disgust at the pudgy man across from her. The cold metal of the handcuffs connecting her to the steel table made her joints ache. She wished for a daydream, while she waited for him to finish staring between her and his clipboard.

"Let's try this again," he flipped a page, "I confirmed your name at the diner, Emily. You say your name is Gwen now. Please, stop wasting my time and state your name for the record."

Emily smiled. "I'd rather not, sir. After all, you haven't introduced yourself properly, either."

He gave a knowing smile some adults got when they thought a child acted especially stupid.

"You were not easy to get a hold of, Miss Cross," said the man, finally. Was she mistaken, or did he sound impressed?

Apparently, he does know something. Just who is this asshole, and how soon can I punch him in the throat?

Emily grimaced, "And yet, here I am, all gotten a hold of. You must be so proud."

"State your name for the record," he repeated, folding his meaty hands.

She supposed there could be nothing further to gain by lying.

"Emily Cross," she responded.

"Thank you, Emily," he said, tipping his head as though he'd been wearing a hat. His short brown hair swayed with the movement. "I am Special Officer Sean Brodus of the Central Intelligence Agency. Call me Sean, or Officer Brodus."

Emily tilted her head back, sighing.

How the hell am I even on their radar? CIA? Why would they even be looking for me in the first place?

This guy wasn't even impressive for a CIA agent. Weren't those guys supposed to be, like, sleek and buff? Sean Brodus looked like a Hot Pocket pretending to be a human on vacation.

"No disrespect, but you really don't look like an agent to me," Emily said, head tilted.

"You're confused by my appearance," said Sean. "There's a significant difference between reality and fiction, young lady."

"Okay," said Emily. "I know the difference."

He slid a brand-new copy of the novel she'd been reading across the table. The girl on the cover seemed to stare at her, eyes gleaming, same as the creature in the woods behind.

"That's not a bad book. I have a copy of my own. More to the point, there's something the American media does in its depictions of special agents we rather enjoy. They cast all these strapping, young, gym-strong type guys and gals in the roles of investigators. Well, the point of the CIA is actually to blend into the populace. We gather information by being forgettable. By allowing ourselves the benefit of being overlooked."

Emily rolled her eyes at him, "Oh, dear lord. Will you please cut to the chase?"

Sean didn't look upset by her attitude in the slightest. In fact, his smile got wider.

"Okay, Emily. I have questions about the Blue Rock Arsenal facility. And you're going to answer my questions. Now, if you would be so kind as to answer them with some measure of haste, we can end this interview much sooner. And maybe, just maybe, I'll feel inclined to get you the sequel to that novel."

Emily raised an eyebrow, "Throw in a triple bacon cheeseburger meal, and you've got a deal."

He chuckled. "You do seem to be growing fond of those, I see. Must have been a limited diet in the facility?"

She shrugged. "Not limited, so much as tailored. Calories and protein, with nary a drop of real flavor. We were basically given a stipend of what amounted to MREs and taught not to run ourselves out of food."

"I see. And how did they enforce it?"

"I don't know you well enough. I'm not sharing that." She looked absently at her wrists. She could swear the rope marks were still there. The damn handcuffs weren't a kind reminder either. She stretched as much as she could, feeling phantom pains where the whip would have struck her back. Remembering her weakness, her humiliation, made her livid. Emily fought against the impulse urging her to scream and beat the life out of the man in front of her.

Sean looked significantly more serious now. "How many of you were there?"

"Last count before they kicked me out, about fifteen. Not counting me or the four dead ones. If I remember right, they started with a roster of roughly twenty candidates."

He said, "Who were the deaths?"

Emily tried to think back. She hadn't known the two in the other group. But the other Nomad candidate had been another girl. She couldn't quite remember her name. Such an unusual name should have popped up like a jack-in-the-box.

After a few moments, it came to her. "Sibyl." She blurted, "Sibyl Mylonas. She was the older sister of a Special Operations Unit member. The other one, can't remember his name, but he died in training. I can't remember the other two at all. They weren't in my unit. Both boys, though."

"How many units were there?"

"Two. The Special Operations Unit, and the Nomad Task Group. And, before you ask, The Nomad Task Group is being pared down to five members, with the rest filtering back into the Special Operations Unit; supposedly keeping them around fifteen members. All except me, that is. I have no idea where they were going to take me."

He looked overly concerned for a moment, picking up the briefcase his clipboard came from. He rifled through a short stack of similar clipboards and looked at one in particular.

"Your mother. Was she-?"

"Yep. Killed in a home invasion when I was four. Right in front of me and Joseph. He would have been seven. Joseph shot the guy with my mom's gun, and we ran. Got picked up by General Blackwood a few hours later and taken to the Arsenal."

"Blackwood?" he asked. "As in, Darius Blackwood?"

She tilted her head. "Yeah, why?"

He shook his head. "It's just something I need to follow up on."

Sean scratched at his clean-shaven chin.

"How much do you know about the other candidates?"

Emily shrugged. "Not a lot. We were rather 'encouraged' not to discuss how we came to be there."

"So, nobody shared with you?"

She gestured with a hand and a raised eyebrow, as if to say, take a guess.

He sighed. "They did, but you didn't care enough to retain that information?"

"Not really. Just thought you could sweat a question of your own. I'm tied up and bored out of my mind."

She sighed and said, "Valko and Nikifor were in a car accident, Maurice got kidnapped by human traffickers, and

Antoine got arrested for accidentally shooting his dad in the woods."

He tapped a pencil on the table. "And Sybil?"

"Now, she never shared. After training one day, she managed to sneak a gun into the locker room and shot herself."

Sean's face fell at the news. "I see."

She said, "They didn't pick us out of a hat. Every one of us got pulled from a family with a military background."

An eyebrow lifted, Sean eyed her. "How do you know that?"

She rolled her eyes. "Enough people in the group mentioned one military branch or the other while discussing how we came to be there. Not happy conversations, to be sure, but it's not hard to see the pattern there."

Sean scratched something on his clipboard, rubbing his chin, eyes narrowed. He flipped a few pages, looking at some other notes, then back to the page he'd been taking notes on.

"Do you have any insight on what Blackwood was trying to accomplish with this program?" He punctuated his question with a tap of his pen on the clipboard.

"He didn't work alone. There were two scientists who ran a bunch of...tests on us. That's the best I can give you."

He said, "Can you give me names? That may help."

"Osric Richards and Wayde Harper. And before you ask, I can't tell you why they did it. All I really know is we each have a demon or two to contend with. And Blackwood helped us to find it, to focus it into action." She finished by pointing a finger at her temple.

Sean frowned but nodded. "About the attack on you at the diner..."

Emily smiled. "Let me guess, you gonna tell me it wasn't just random violence? Look at you, investigating."

"You may find this amusing, but I don't. We identified some of the bodies. The girl I saw shooting at you was missing, but I suspect she was working with a terrorist group calling themselves, 'Alcyde's Hounds'."

"And that's a problem because…"

He pulled a file from his briefcase and started laying out glossy photographs. Each one had a face and a closeup of a distinct shoulder tattoo. A blood-red hound above a silvery curved dagger. One showed a group on a sidewalk. One in the middle of a forest clearing. Another appeared to be taken in some sort of dingy warehouse. And then, she saw the pale lime-colored carpet her mother had picked out. She'd never seen such a vibrant green, paired with such an ugly, multicolored sofa. And she could never forget it, either. She ignored the bodies covered in blood. She never forgot those faces and didn't need the reminder.

"Over fifteen bodies identified with that marking. We know little to nothing about them, but they're somehow connected to almost every one of the children we've identified as having been recruited into the Blue Rock ROTC program." He said the word 'recruited' while gesturing air quotes. "The only one we have definitive information on is Antoine's father. But he vanished after imprisonment until his death. His dishonorable discharge from the SEALs is the only link we have."

Emily tossed her hair back as best she could with her hands shackled. She blew at a stubborn strand tickling the bridge of her nose and grunted at it. It stayed in front of her eye, annoying her to no end.

"I think I see what you're doing, then," said Emily. "And I want to help you get them out."

Sean smiled. "You're already helping. With what you've told me, I can get a task force into the Arsenal to extract your friends."

Emily rolled her eyes. "Raids never go the way you guys think. I've seen enough reports to know that much, and I'd rather have a chance to warn my brother before the shooting starts."

His eyes narrowed. "What you're really saying is you don't trust me."

Emily scoffed. "Hell no, I don't trust you. You're not benching me on this."

"Emily, I need you to understand something," he said, his smile hinting at frustration. "This is not a negotiation. I'm sending in a team, and that's all there is to it."

Emily seethed behind clenched teeth. In a way, she understood that kid, Steven, better now. He wouldn't sit there and take this. He'd do...something. Probably punch someone. He would fight his way out and make his way on his own. And when he finished, he would quietly accept whatever punishment those in charge deemed appropriate. Emily believed with all certainty; she'd survived worse in Blue Rock than anything these agents would be willing to do to her.

Having come to her conclusion, Emily closed her eyes and took in a deep, calming breath. She released the breath as she opened her eyes, looking into the stern, smiling face of Special Agent Sean Brodus.

"Fine," she said. "I'll stop asking. Can I have a cheeseburger now? I'm about to add to my list of demands if you don't let me eat soon."

"We'll see." He stood, stacking his papers together and carrying them to the door. Her novel still lay on the table, just out of reach.

Well? I'm not begging for the damn book. I'll just get another one.

Sean rapped at the door. Another agent came in, unlocking the cuffs holding Emily to the steel table. The woman closed the cuffs back around Emily's wrists, and Sean gestured for them to follow.

Sean tapped the papers in his hands and made a show of glancing at his wristwatch. "You coming? I've still got to get you to Jersey."

Emily glanced at both agents. "You're taking me back to Blue Rock so I can help."

Sean looked away for a moment. He pinched the bridge of his nose and took a deep breath. When he looked back, his expression turned hard and cold.

"Little girl," he said. "You may not understand this, but there are some bad people who want you and your friends very dead right now. I'm doing everything in my power to keep you alive. I'm trying to save you, your brother, and your friends. Stop pretending you're stupid and get your ass in gear."

Emily glared back at him. "Call me little girl again, asshole. Give me one reason to wreck your shit."

"What are you not understanding here? You are in my custody. You aren't in a position to threaten me." Sean folded his arms and suddenly it became a stand-off.

Emily smiled. "Think so, huh? Do you even know what they trained us for?"

He gazed at her curiously. "Does it matter what they trained you for? The entire operation is illegal."

"Richards and Blackwood have an army of monsters in that base," she explained.

"You're not monsters. You're kids," Sean said, turning to walk on. He motioned for her to follow.

Emily stared at the back of his head, not moving despite the gentle hand pushing at her elbow. "And you're not listening. I'm not talking about us. I'm talking about biological weapons."

Sean stopped, turning on his heel, eyes narrowed. "Explain."

She whispered at first, memories of the monsters causing an involuntary shiver. "They made us fight them; called them Talon-types. And they have claws capable of tearing holes in level four body armor."

Emily scratched at the bridge of her nose awkwardly. "And the longer they're active, the smarter they get. They learn to hunt in packs. They get downright tactical after just a few hours."

"Why are you sharing this now?" Sean glanced at the other agent and concern hardened his features.

Emily said, "Because, otherwise, you're going to get a bunch of your trigger-happy agents killed for no reason, against creatures you can't begin to comprehend. And, right now, my brother's life is in your hands. I don't mean any disrespect, but I don't trust you."

Sean folded his arms again. An annoying gesture, to be sure. "That makes me glad I'm not supposed to take you. At the same time, our field agents know what they're doing."

Emily glowered. "I'd appreciate you getting me out of these handcuffs, so I can fix my hair and feel halfway like a human being, instead of your little ginger puppy on a string." Emily held out her cuffed wrists.

I'm done asking to be on your task force. Either you're taking me with you, or I'll find a way out of your custody and make my own way there.

Sean pressed his lips into a thin line. He squinted his beady brown eyes as he absently tapped the stack of papers in his hand. He sneered at her and let out an exasperated sigh, fishing in his pocket.

"What you just told me sounds like a load of crap," he said.

Emily smirked. "Believe what you want to. If I needed to lie to you, you couldn't tell the difference."

He snorted derisively as he pulled a handcuff key from his pocket. He sighed again.

"Look," he said. "We can take the cuffs off. But behave yourself. My hands are tied on the orders to get you away from these people."

Shrugging, Emily offered her wrists up. She was honestly a bit amazed. He likely knew the risk he was taking, removing the cuffs. As soon as her hands were free, she pulled her hair into a ponytail and breathed a sigh of relief.

He's not so bad, I guess. Who knows? Maybe he'll actually get me that burger.

7 The Road

Among the foliage behind the church, Steven nearly punched Curtis at the other boy's sudden motion of jumping up from beside a nearby tree.

Curtis said, "I thought you said you shot Dr. Harper."

Steven spun on his heel, bringing up the Glock in a smooth motion. Wayde Harper's skin was as red as raw meat, his face contorted, and his silver hair now matted with drying blood. Both hands had sprouted claws. He only wore one shoe. On closer inspection, the bullet wounds looked scabbed over.

"What the hell?" Steven whispered. "Guys, get moving. When I start shooting, we're going to have a lot of company very fast."

The rest of the group jumped to their feet, Brice lifting Pattie. They ran as Steven faced off against Harper.

Harper growled. "You're all impure, pathetic creatures, Mr. Fuller. I thought you'd be proud of my handiwork. Don't you like my new body? It's better now, in every way."

Steven steadied his aim, a thousand thoughts shoving their way through his brain. A million explanations, none of which made sense. He'd shot this man twice in the chest. His heart and lung should have ruptured at the very least.

Watching the others retreat from the corner of his eye, Steven tried to hold Harper's attention. "How, exactly, are you still alive?"

Harper tapped a claw to his chin, showing a shark-toothed grin. "I suppose you've earned something by killing me once. I didn't let Richards program my dose of the virus, so I'm not driven to kill. Unless I want to. Which, I really do, of course. I wonder if you'll survive long enough to find your answers."

"Who the hell is Richards? And, what's that got to do with me?"

"Leave it to an experiment not to know the parameters."

"You're still hesitating, Steven," said his father's voice. They were out at a range. Steven stood holding his father's pistol, trembling; afraid of the power he'd just witnessed from it.

Steven narrowed his eyes. "So, I'm somehow tied to these monsters?"

Not just tied to; I am a monster. I've known it all along.

The euphoria that came from every hit. The exhilarating frenzy from his gun's recoil pushing back toward his body.

Harper's smile got impossibly wider, the skin around his lips splitting, revealing the muscle beneath. "You're so close to the answer, I can feel it. It's so...rewarding to watch students work through their problems and find the solutions."

"I won't lie to you, Steven." Father knelt beside him, pressing an ice pack to a purpling bruise on Steven's face. "There's going to come a day when I'm not with you. You'll still have to stand on your feet and move your ass."

Steven breathed and centered his aim. Harper tilted his head, the smile never fading. He moved too fast. Ducking down, Harper rushed forward, swiping out with his clawed hand. Steven took no time to think as he leaped back and hit his shoulder on a tree. The unintentional stumble saved his life, as Harper's claw dug into the wood of the magnolia.

Harper ripped his claw free, the back of his hand smacking against Steven's face. Steven's vision went black for just a few moments, and he heard an incredible ringing in his ear. He shook his head clear and instinctively dropped to the ground, rolling. The claw hit another tree, bone, and wood cracking against one another.

Holy crows, I'm not dead yet. I will be if I don't get off the defense and start fighting back.

Steven jumped back to his feet, vision clear, and turned to Harper, firing. His first shot hit Harper in the shoulder. The second hit the chest, and Harper staggered. The third shot just clicked. Nothing happened. Harper charged him.

Steven's heart hammered in his chest. The damn thing was jammed. Standing firm, he tapped the Glock's magazine with his free palm and racked the slide to chamber a new round. It still didn't work.

Harper lunged forward, his growl deepening, plunging his claws ahead of him. Steven ducked in toward Harper, grabbed what remnants were left of the man's shirt, and dropped backward. He used Harper's momentum against him, sending the monster face-first into a hedgerow.

When he removed the magazine, the slide immediately cycled forward. Harper extricated himself from the bushes and turned around with a snarl as Steven finished reinserting the magazine. Steven fired once, the bullet piercing through to the back of Harper's head.

Half slumped with dread, Steven took a mental note of the situation they faced. Three bullets were all that stood between his ragtag group and the perils of the next two miles of city they needed to cover.

He took off after the others, the growls of nearby creatures rising behind him. *They must have heard the scuffle and subsequent gunshots.* He shuddered to think about the implications of Harper's words. But he couldn't stop considering the situation any more than he could stop the tragedy playing out around him.

Why the hell did Pattie have to be right about this? A two-mile walk had never looked longer.

They had barely begun their journey to the safe house. He was running out of ammunition. Pattie and Mirena had injuries slowing them down. He didn't know how many magazines Pattie brought, but she had the only other gun in the group. Maybe Brice could use Pattie's gun to keep them covered on at least one other side.

I don't know if I can trust Curtis with a gun. The stress is making him crack. I mean, he's always been high-strung, but I'll have to be careful not to rely on him too much.

Steven swayed on his feet, the pain in his face a dull ache. He pushed through as the world spun around him. His head pounded, and his ear still rang. He stopped a moment, touching a finger to the side of his head. His hand came away bloody. *Inner ear damage.* He would be off-balance for hours, at least. It would affect his aim if he let it distract him.

He broke out of the tree line at the next street, the group appearing just ahead. Pattie was walking on her own again, though with a pronounced limp. From a distance, it appeared that Brice was carrying her gun. Steven would have smiled at the fortune, if there wasn't a pair of monsters creeping along near the group, using the stopped cars as cover.

Running forward on aching feet, Steven hoped beyond hope that he would make it in time. Movement registered in his peripheral vision, but Steven couldn't tell who at this speed. He focused on the targets ahead. The monsters would pounce any moment. As he thought it, they bounded over the cars, rushing toward the group. Brice didn't see them. He turned too late.

Adrenaline wouldn't be enough. Steven's chest tightened, replacing heartbeats with a pulsing pain. Steven felt as though ice coursed through his lungs instead of oxygen as he sprinted. One of the monsters turned, startled and snarling, as he ran in close.

Without slowing his pace, Steven thrust the Glock into the monster's chin and pulled the trigger, just before his momentum took him into the waiting arms of the second creature. Its arms wrapped him tightly. With a swift movement, it squeezed.

Steven screamed as the monster crushed him. Something broke inside him, and claws pierced his sides. He struggled, but the thing had an ironclad hold on him. He forced his arm around, aiming blindly, and pulled the trigger. The bullet scraped across the side of its head. He shot again, the slide locking back. The shot missed but passed less than an inch from its ear. The monster howled, lifted him high, and threw him to the ground.

He no longer screamed. He could get no more breath to scream. Vision swimming, he pointed his empty gun with trembling, barely stable hands. Nothing happened when he squeezed the trigger in a desperate reaction to the pain. A gun reported, but it wasn't his. He let it drop with no strength left in his fingers to pull the trigger. He had burned through the last of his adrenaline, and his body was catching up to reality.

As his vision faded, he saw the monster ahead of him fall to the ground, shuddering once. Brice and Nyura stood over him moments later, Brice holding Pattie's pistol, sweeping the street to cover them. Nyura knelt beside Steven. Fingers pressed into Steven's neck.

She's checking to see if I'm in shock. Say something, dammit! Why the hell can't I breathe right? I've run harder than this in training.

Nyura pulled another of the small cylinders from her pouch. 'Look, this is my last painkiller, and I only kept the one tampon on me. You just had to get stabbed by the claws, didn't you?"

Cutting away his shirt with her small knife, she shook her head. Her eyes went wide at the sight of his chest and she sucked in a breath. "I mean, seriously, boy. What the hell are you made of?"

She used the pieces that weren't already soaked in blood to make makeshift bandages, tying them about his midsection, yanking the ends to ensure they were tight. A fresh wave of pain washed over him, and he sucked in an agonized breath.

"Congratulations, you're breathing again," she said with a placating smile. "Don't sing my praises now, though. I owe you one too many so far."

Steven squeezed his eyes shut against the burning in his sides and ribs. Something pricked his skin, and a moment later, a cooling sensation spread throughout his body. He lay there for what seemed an egregious amount of time.

Opening his eyes, he reached out to the outstretched hands of Nyura and Brice. He struggled to keep his feet under him as he pushed out of their grips. Nyura protested, but Steven shook his head, forcing himself to move through the stiffness in his muscles. He glanced toward Grace and Mirena as he picked up his empty Glock and put it in a pocket. They were safe, holding onto one another for support.

He moved on unsteady legs, though strength began returning to his limbs. "We need to keep moving."

Curtis snorted, speaking under his breath to Ladeen. "I wish it had killed him. Save me the trouble."

Steven narrowed his eyes and snatched Curtis's shirt, pulling both of them almost completely off their feet. He only swayed a little, feeling a warm trickle of blood from his mouth, the acrid taste all but overpowering him as he slammed Curtis bodily into a car. The blood must have come from something broken within.

"Stop. It." he growled in Curtis's face. "Stop giving me reasons, dammit. I don't want to waste any more of our limited time with your hatred."

Steven breathed heavily. Curtis's dark eyes bore into him with vehement hostility.

"You owe me some apologies," spat Curtis.

Steven glared back. "I don't care what you think I owe you. Where you feel inadequate is neither my fault, nor is it my responsibility. But all your dissent stops right now."

"Because you say so, right?" Curtis swallowed, clenching his jaw and glaring.

Steven said, "You haven't even guessed at the real difference between us."

Sneering, Curtis said, "Oh yeah, killer? And what's that?"

Steven's free hand went instinctively to his chest. "I've died once already. I'm not apologizing to a simple-minded fool too deluded to understand where his actual enemies are."

"You going to kill me and get it over with, then?" Curtis's voice somehow seemed firmer than before.

In a flash, Steven held Curtis by the throat. The other boy's eyes went wide as saucers as he clawed at the tightening grip with one hand, his efforts useless.

Steven smiled. A dark smile, full of violent intent. "Your optimism is adorable. Keep tempting me, let's see how long I hold out."

Curtis whimpered, thrashing to try and draw breath. His eyes glazed over. Nyura and Brice pulled at Steven. Weakened from his injuries, he loosened his grip, letting Curtis take in a little air. He glared at the other two. Brice put his hands up, backing away.

Steven sighed. "I don't know how or why I came back. I must have lost a little over two liters of blood when paramedics found me. I died on the table in the emergency room. I saw a darkness that you can't begin to comprehend."

Curtis fell to his knees as Steven released the grip.

"You'll never beat me. I fight for every breath I take. Every heartbeat. For every single person I have the power to keep safe from that darkness. That includes you, even if you hate me."

Curtis choked a little, spluttering. "That doesn't make you special. Like you said before, we've all been in the dark. You're no more important than the rest of us."

Steven gripped Curtis by the hair and yanked him to his feet. A gentle reminder. "Get in line, and do your job. Or find your own way, and get the hell out of mine. If you can't live with those options, I'm more than willing to kill you with a smile on my face."

He released his grip, and Curtis dropped to the ground, panting and wheezing. Ladeen, Mirena, and Grace stared at Steven, slack-jawed and wide-eyed. The other operatives glared at Curtis.

Nyura cleared her throat. "Can this be over? We do need to keep going. We need better medical supplies for the wounded, and a resupply of ammunition. Are you sure you're good to walk, Steven?"

Grunting, Steven gave her a thumbs up. "I'll be fine."

"Fine?" Brice looked incredulous. "We have very different definitions of the word, I think."

Steven ignored Brice's attempt at a joke and started walking. Trudging, more like.

"Was that necessary?" Grace walked beside Steven, flinching at every other noise.

Almost seems like she's flinching with every move I make. I went too far. Today is a damned disaster and a half.

The group walked on in silence, Curtis trailing behind with a hand in his pocket and his head hung low. Pain welled in Steven's heart at the words he'd used. But he also couldn't let Curtis undermine their efforts. When survival became a question, the petty squabbles needed to be put aside. Otherwise, only one answer awaited them.

Steven heaved a sigh. "As unfortunate as it is, yes. Every time we have to stop to deal with his attitude, it's time we should be using to get you three someplace safer."

"So..." She hesitated. "All those threats were for us?"

Steven said, "I can't speak for everyone here. For my part, yes. I couldn't save everyone. But I have the opportunity to save you."

Grace put a hand on his arm. The touch brought a gentle, soft warmth to his skin. He welcomed it, letting it melt his stress. "If your mission is to save all our lives, stop threatening his."

He ran a hand through his hair, rubbing at the sweaty locks. "He's putting you in danger."

She squeezed lightly. "I understand you think that. Have you stopped to think maybe he's scared, too?"

Steven groaned as he turned to look at her. "So, I should just let him lash out at me? I'm a little confused as to what you want me to do here. He's been picking fights with me over the better part of the last five years. If this had been just today's issue, I'd have no problem seeing it from your angle."

Her eyes, bright in the afternoon sun, softened his expression. He exhaled a heavy sigh.

She said, "What I'm saying is to consider your priorities and pick your battles. What he's doing ultimately doesn't matter, if it doesn't actively put us in harm's way, right? So, get us to the place, and deal with your frustrations there. Why waste energy on his pettiness, when it's the same energy you need to use to fight?"

Steven couldn't help it. His face broke into a nervous smile. His heart hammered in his chest. "I have to admit, you make a solid point. Suddenly, I wish I'd paid more attention to you all along. I could get used to you counseling me."

She paused for a moment, blinking rapidly. A light blush spread across her cheeks, and she turned away. Steven could swear she kept stealing glances.

Smoke rising on the horizon ahead gave him reason to be on edge. Steven slipped, stumbling a moment before catching himself against a stopped car. His head spun again, but he shook it and pushed on. She reached out to grab him. He held her hand and steadied himself.

"When we get you home," he said, slowly, "I have something I need to check on."

Grace narrowed her eyes. "When you get me home, you need to rest. You're barely even standing right now."

He said, "I need to know how widespread this infection is. I need to know what it is. Harper made it sound like this was some kind of disease. Nothing he said made sense, but if he told the truth about it, maybe I can find some answers at the Arsenal."

Someone tapped Steven's shoulder. He turned to Brice, who held out a closed hand. He cleared his throat and playfully eyed his own hand until Steven put out a hand to receive whatever prize it contained.

Brice dropped twelve rounds of nine-millimeter ammunition into Steven's hand, smiling. "This is the last from Pattie's extra mags. I've got five left in the twenty-six, and you're a better shot with a pistol. You good to get us to the safe house, sir?"

Steven rolled his eyes. "The hell is this 'sir' business?"

Brice held his hands up again. "Yeah. Not arguing to run point. You're leading, like it or not."

Steven smiled again. "No pressure, right?"

Brice's dark brown eyes gleamed. "Nah. The pressure comes when I get a rifle in my hands. Then, we'll see if you can keep up."

Steven laughed. It hurt like hell, but he laughed and enjoyed it. He took the magazine from his Glock and seated the rounds. Replacing the magazine in the pistol, he racked the slide, chambering one. It felt better having it loaded and ready to go. The long walk ahead almost seemed shorter because of it.

8 Proximity

Valko squeezed the hilt of one of the two knives strapped to his chest plate. He wondered at the scene before him as he fitted shells into the drum magazine for his shotgun. These people had just...changed. Shifted. Like a switch somewhere had been flipped, and now they were bloodthirsty maniacs with claws for fingers.

This doesn't make any damn sense.

He and the other four Nomads stood, fully armored, in the midst of fifteen Talon-type corpses. The gunmetal gray shone in the afternoon sun. Each young man looked at the others, in turn. Each checked their equipment once again in preparation. The driving gate to the Arsenal compound stood open, revealing a destitute city filled with smoke and broken cars.

"Communicators and cell towers are down," said Joseph, his voice somewhat distorted through his helmet. "When we get them back online, code names over the radio only."

Antoine piped up, "What's the point? Who's gonna listen in? The Talons?"

Joseph turned slowly. "That's always been the protocol, though it was routinely ignored during training. Given that this is a real situation, we're going to follow orders as given."

"Why not just...go?" Antoine gestured in a random direction, his other hand cradling a massive rifle.

Please do.

Joseph groaned. "And this is why I wish you were the one kicked out."

If anyone could have seen through his helmet, Antoine would have been sneering. Valko could imagine it with little difficulty. He needed to do something. Joseph was already gripping his sub-machine gun a little tighter than Valko considered healthy.

Nikifor raised a hand. "So, what are our orders, Cross?"

Valko breathed a quiet sigh of relief. He could always count on Nikifor to think of the best way to move forward. Although, if he were honest, he was envious of that ability. On the whole, however, the mission was already screwed.

The Nomads might be used to fighting Talons, but civilians wouldn't stand a chance. He had his doubts about the Special Operations members, like Steven. Maybe they could hold out for a while, but eventually, the Talons would out-flank them. The damn things were too adaptable.

Joseph turned back to the rest of the group. He pointed at himself and Maurice. "Wisp and I are headed to the comms building. He should be able to get them back online."

Pointing at Nikifor, he said, "Webb will run reconnaissance, noting any pockets of survivors in need of extraction."

Finally, he turned to Antoine and Valko. "Country Mile and Proximity will extract survivors as needed and sequester them here at the Arsenal."

"Are we expecting reinforcements?" said Nikifor. "Seems a waste to bring all those people to such a central point, given what's out there. I'd hate to bring them back to die here."

Joseph said, "We can hold here as needed, and house civilians in the special operations dormitory. Abaroa went against Blackwood's orders and tried to get a call out to the Arkansas National Guard. No word on whether he got through to them before the lines went down."

Nikifor tilted his armored head. "And all communications magically went out after he disobeyed orders?"

Joseph hesitated. "I was in the room when Abaroa disobeyed orders. Blackwood was pissed, but he wasn't in a position to do anything about it. Too many people changed at once, and we had to fight our way out to the command wing. Not sure how they're getting along right now, but we have a mission. Comms going down was separate and unrelated to the argument."

Valko shrugged. "So do we know why comms failed or not?"

"Negative," said Joseph. "But, according to Abaroa, it must have had something to do with that science teacher. Doctor Harper. No word on his whereabouts, but if you see him, orders are to capture, though lethal force is authorized if he's uncooperative."

Antoine shouldered the rifle. "We gonna keep talkin' about it, or are we doing something?"

Joseph stared through the armored glass visor of his helmet.

Well, this is about to turn into a slush pile. After what happened with Emily, I want to kill him. Why the hell is he pushing his luck?

"Be honest, 'Cross'," Antoine said, using his free hand to gesture in quotations. "On a scale from one to ten, how bad do you want to shoot me right now?"

"I'm hovering somewhere in the high thirties," said Joseph. "Want to stop being an asshole and do your job?"

Antoine laughed a hearty belly laugh, turning toward the arsenal gates. "Nah. I'mma do my job, alright. But, you and I know I'll never stop being an asshole. Life just wouldn't be the same if I did. Kind of like if I ever got rid of my dulcet tones, y'know?"

"Whatever," Joseph said with a dismissive wave. "Move out, Nomads. Let's save some lives."

Valko walked with Antoine and Nikifor out the front gates of the Arsenal. As they passed into the city itself, the afternoon air crackled with tension.

"Something stinks about this whole situation," said Nikifor, his voice edged with frustration.

Valko perked up. "Like 'a lab contract worker being able to turn people into Talon-types' stinks?"

Nikifor shook his head. "No. It goes deeper than that. Why didn't we change with the rest of the staff? Why didn't Blackwood or Abaroa? Exactly how many Talon-types are we looking at in the city?"

Antoine put an arm around Nikifor, earning a glare. "Because we're made of stronger stuff than the everyday namby-pambies. At least, I think that's how my daddy said it."

Shoving the arm off, Nikifor's voice was cold. "I don't know who you think you are, but I have enough reasons to want you dead without you touching me."

Putting up a hand, Antoine backed away a couple of steps. Valko could imagine the shark-toothed grin behind the opaque black helmet visor. Antoine just had this way about him. Especially since Emily had left. He would say and do things just to get under everyone's skin.

Valko assumed it was because he liked watching how people reacted to the provocation. The only problem here was, considering the strain between them, none of the other Nomads would care about having to leave Antoine behind as a corpse. And, on some level, one of them being the cause of death didn't give him any pause either.

Shaking his head, Nikifor continued. "Whatever we're walking into, I feel like Blackwood's involved."

Valko shrugged. "Hell of a theory, Niki. But does that even matter right now?"

"It very much matters. We're under his command, and he doesn't want us to receive reinforcements," said Nikifor.

Antoine aimed his rifle toward a rooftop as they trudged along. "It's because we're enough. We don't need help."

Nikifor shook his head, the web motif of his armor seeming to shift patterns with the movement. "That kind of thinking is going to get someone killed. We're good, but we're five against a potential twelve thousand or so targets. On top of that, we have to get another significant portion of that populace back to relative safety at the Arsenal. It's a simple numbers game. They have more."

Something about Nikifor's tone stirred in Valko's mind. Valko looked at Nikifor's visor. "That's not the worst of it, is it?"

Pausing to take a deep breath, Nikifor's shoulders drooped. "Of course, it isn't. Who knows how many Akuma-types there are mixed into the population."

With a shudder, Valko sucked in a sharp breath. "I hadn't thought about that."

Antoine tilted his head. "The hell are y'all talking about now?"

"The Akuma-type monsters," said Nikifor. "They're faster, stronger. And, unless you absolutely destroy them, their regeneration is off the charts."

"Why have I not known about this?" asked Antoine, incredulous.

Valko scoffed. "You're a sniper with an anti-materiel rifle. At what point would you be close enough to the enemy to care about the differences?"

Shrugging, Antoine scanned another roof with his rifle. "Good point. I do reckon you boys might need to know more than I would."

Antoine's rifle reported, and the body of a Talon-type monster fell from the roof. Looking up, Valko saw where the fifty caliber round had torn through bricks to hit the creature.

"Well, our position is clear to the enemy now," Nikifor said in a disinterested fashion as howls erupted around them in the afternoon air.

"The official answer," said Nikifor. "You, Maurice, and Emily simply weren't ready. An Akuma-type is a completely different category in terms of challenge. Joseph, Valko, and myself are the only Nomad candidates rated to face one, and it nearly killed the three of us, together."

Antoine chuckled, scanning the horizon. "Well, if we run into any, I'll let the two of you handle it. I'll just sit back and do what I do best."

So, you'll talk it to death. Lord knows it's working on me.

Nikifor sighed, moving faster to get ahead. "Yeah. You do that."

A growl sounded to the right and Valko whipped around to face it. A Talon-type leapt from the shadows of an alley. He lifted his shotgun level with the creature's chest and fired. The slug punched into its torso. It dropped to the ground, quivering.

Nikifor reached an intersection and turned, firing his rifle in five rapid snaps. He raised a hand and gestured for them to follow. Valko and Antoine hustled forward, taking up a position at the intersection.

The body of a Talon-type lay across a stopped car. Four others were randomly sprawled along the asphalt. A human body slumped in the driver's seat of the car, a spattering of blood dripping down the cracked windshield. Nikifor waved, and four people cautiously emerged from an alley behind the car.

Valko lowered his aim and waved the people over. The sound of Talons approaching spurred him into motion. He and Antoine led them back toward the main street as the sun dipped in the sky, casting a burning orange aura over the world around him.

9 The Scars Within

Steven groaned through the pain as he checked his phone's display. The screen was shattered on one side, but he could still see the time. They had been walking for just over thirty-five minutes. They were close to the safe house. Nyura and Ladeen carried Pattie between them, draped as she was. She kept slipping in and out of consciousness.

We're so close. Close enough that everything can fall apart right here and now. Is it too much to hope--that we make it?

Steven shook his head, fighting against vertigo from his damaged ear. "Nyura. How's Pattie doing?"

Nyura frowned. "She's too pale. I'm getting worried. But if we get there soon, there should be enough equipment to get her properly patched up. You, too, for that matter."

He forced a smile. "Good. Let me know when we're there. I didn't even know these safe houses existed before today."

Nyura half attempted a shrug. He saw uncertainty in the way she avoided his gaze. "Need-to-know basis, and all that crap, I guess."

Eye scrunched, Nyura moved a strand of hair out of Pattie's face. She felt the other girl's forehead and appeared to deflate a bit.

"We'll make it," said Steven. "You'll save her."

Nyura's eyes glistened as she turned her pinched face to him. "Stop lying to yourself. I think you know our chances better than anyone else here."

He shook his head, putting a hand out to lean on a stopped car. His head still spun. He could swear someone kept tilting the earth away from him, moment by moment. "You've always been so damn confident. I can't imagine what Pattie means to you. But you are not allowed to doubt yourself. Not when we're this close. It's not over until we're dead. And, if I'm any indication, even that may not stick."

Metal crunched behind them. Steven spun on his heels, grating against the stabbing, burning pain in his sides. His vision spun a bit faster, and a wave of nausea swept over him. He stepped around the group to clear a firing line and lifted the Glock. The sight of Wayde Harper standing atop a crushed car froze his blood. The hole on Harper's face was crusted over and dark. Harper snarled and roared. It was an impossibly feral sound for a human body to make.

What the hell? Headshots have been enough to drop these things. I can't fight this bastard straight on a second time.

Eyes frantically searching the area, Curtis backed away. "Uh, you were saying?"

Monsters rushed in from several alleys. It was a tightening vise of claws and dark intent. Five so far, not counting Harper. Brice took up a firing position as the others gathered into a tight knot. Curtis lifted Pattie into his arms with effort as the group began moving.

Mirena muttered, "Not again,"

"Nyura." Steven didn't take his eyes away from Harper as he breathed in, attempting to slow his heart rate. "Where, exactly, is the safe house?"

Nyura was already guiding the group toward an empty side street. Her voice was strained, almost broken. "It's just another block. Haven Self-Storage. Building Echo, Unit 201. Scan your ID at the pedestrian gate to get in."

The monsters roared, twisting their bodies. Moving to surround the group. He shifted his aim to an approaching creature. Steven fired, but it had been watching. It shifted its stance just as he committed to the trigger pull. "Brice! You're on point. Get them there!"

Brice nodded, wide-eyed, as the group moved. He stayed toward the rear to guard, then ran ahead as Steven got the attention of the monsters with another shot. It hit one in the leg.

Steven growled through gritted teeth. "I don't have nearly enough time or bullets for this."

He pulled his gun back into the close quarters firing position. He wondered if he could possibly survive them surrounding him. Steven had some serious doubts about that, considering the circumstances.

Have enough time. Get there. Where the hell is Harper?

Movement behind a wrecked truck. Something was attempting to flank him from the other side.

Something awakened within Steven. A feeling he normally dreaded. An excitement that he admitted shame in knowing. That drive within led him to challenge those he knew to be stronger. An innate, carnal desire. Fight. Kill. Survive. His range of vision expanded to take in more of the movement around him as his breathing evened out into a smooth rhythm.

Adrenaline took over. He smiled as he tilted the gun and fired into the face of a lunging monster less than a few feet away. As it dropped, a certain kind of clarity emerged.

Steven watched in a quiet terror as his father pulled a concealed pistol and shot a couple of his attackers. The men seemed to have come out of nowhere. And it had been such a beautiful day. A man with a knife slipped in close enough from behind, grabbing Steven's father by the head, plunging his knife into father's back. Three times.

Father fell to the sidewalk, blood pouring from him like someone had turned the handle on a faucet. Some of the blood from his upper back was frothing and pink. He didn't know what it meant back then. Steven had no idea his father's lung was punctured and collapsing. All he remembered was screaming. Crying.

Steven spun with a sudden blow from the side, forcing himself to ignore the claws that sliced his skin. He fired into the monster's snarling face. It was hard to miss when they were this close. He breathed in a slow rhythm as he pivoted on his feet, shooting as they closed in.

The man had turned around at the scream. He had no expression on his face as he swung the knife down, its already bloody edge gouging a path from Steven's collarbone to the lowest of his ribs. He'd just stood there. Why hadn't he moved? Done something? His arm hung loosely, and he could see the white of his clavicle showing through as blood filled the space and spilled out onto his bright yellow shirt. Steven felt nothing but fear; not even the pain, though it burned brighter than the sun above.

His pulse raced. Bile rose in his throat as he spun, eyes landing on faces just before his bullets found their marks. His lungs were too heavy, his head too light. Bright spots clouded his vision, and his gut roiled with the constant motion. But he kept moving. Kept shooting.

And then, something strange happened. Steven's father rose, blood spilling from his body. He turned, face contorted. And with fury in his eyes, slammed his fist into the side of the attacking man's head. The man's head twisted from the impact, and Steven remembered the sickening crack as the man dropped, his face frozen in pain. The light fading from his eyes.

Steven's father fell again, not moving. Steven didn't know when he lost consciousness and fell to the ground himself. But it didn't matter. In a way, he was just as dead as if he'd never awakened again. And yet, that final act of defiance from his father had sparked something. An instinct of sorts.

The fragments of memory made Steven's blood boil. He welcomed the coming fight. It was a desire as pure as a wolf's hunger.

Why should I deny my nature? I am a warrior, like my father before me. I remember your favorite quote, Dad. It belongs to me now. I took your blood. Your fury. Your resolve. Now I am become Death, the destroyer of worlds. Wrecker of your shit.

Steven ducked as a red claw swiped by him. Harper snarled, snapping his jaws like an animal. Steven brought his gun up. It was empty again. Panic seized Steven as Harper's claws hurtled towards his face.

Something dark gray smashed into Harper from the side. Steven turned with the movement. He recognized the armor; it was one of the Nomads. As Harper hit the ground, the Nomad lifted a drum-fed shotgun and fired it into Harper's face twice. Harper's corpse lay still yet again. This time, however, without his head.

Steven groaned. "Please, for the sake of all things good and holy, tell me he's actually dead this time."

The Nomad turned Steven's way and he caught a glimpse of the armor decorations. The front plate of a Claymore mine was riveted to either shoulder of the armor. Two knives were holstered on either side of his chest plate, and what looked to be two Kimber forty-five caliber pistols rested in thigh holsters.

Considering the setup, it could only be Valko.

A second Nomad sauntered up a few moments later. He carried a massive rifle, and his armor was unadorned, except for a bullseye etched into the bulletproof glass visor, just over where his right eye would be. *Antoine, maybe?*

Valko was a bit shorter, with a broader chest. The Nomad with the rifle pointed a finger at Steven as though it was a gun and dropped his thumb.

He said, "Bang, puke. You're dead."

Yep. Antoine.

Sitting on the pavement, Steven groaned. "Lucky me."

Valko scanned the area. "An Akuma can't heal without its head. Where'd the others go? Country Mile here saw them with you, but we couldn't shoot while you were surrounded."

"One block north." Steven tried to point in an approximate direction as the world spun around him. He vomited. The deep red color worried him. The way his face seemed to be slowly approaching the mess outside of his control worried him more.

"Damn," said Antoine, from somewhere nearby. "The puke thing was just a joke nickname. You didn't have to go and do it."

"Leave him alone," said Valko. "He's probably killed more Talons today than you. Held his own against an Akuma, too."

Hands grabbed him, lifting him.

"You sound so impressed." Antoine's voice dripped sarcasm. "Didn't look like you had a hard time. I could take one of those lobster-looking dudes, easy."

Country Mile? Sounds like the kind of nickname Joseph would have come up with. Does he just not get the joke? What the hell is a Talon? An Akuma? Did I point them in the right direction?

Valko ignored Antoine's pestering with a grunt. His voice was softer as he said, "I'm sorry we didn't make it to you sooner.

I'm also starting to wonder why you weren't in the program with us."

"You serious?" Antoine said, "I'll admit, the shooting was rather...well, something, at least. Should have shot them from farther away though. Fewer lacerations that way."

"Shut it," Valko growled. "Until you actually take on an Akuma by yourself and live through it, you've got nothing else to say about Steven. You beat him in a spar. When he was already tired. Big deal, tough guy. I guarantee you, if it mattered, he would have killed you outright."

"I'm feelin' real disrespected right now, Proximity. I whooped his ass. Why do you and Cross want to downplay that? Because I got hit once or twice?" Antoine's voice somehow gained even more of its signature twang.

"And?" Valko stopped, turning. Steven could imagine Antoine rolling his eyes.

"Y'know what?" said Antoine. "Screw this mission. Screw you, and the high horse you rode in on. Gettin' real tired of being treated like shit and talked down to."

Valko's hands trembled. A deep growl issued from him. Valko snarled. "After what you did, you want respect? Do you even think that's possible? I only tolerate you because I've been ordered to."

Antoine chuckled. "I see. So, the boy too big for his britches gets beat up, and everybody wants to get mad as a wet hen at me, coming to defend him. I reckon ain't none of you got the good sense God gave a rock!"

Valko's growl deepened. He sounded like an enraged dog. But he kept trudging, helping Steven to take step after agonized step down the street Nyura and the others had taken.

"It is what it is, though, Proximity," Antoine droned, seemingly oblivious. "We'll eventually leave this hole, and live somewhere far away from one another. Probably today. Though, I get the feeling the golden child bleeding from his tummy ache ain't going very much farther."

Steven trembled, feeling the roiling of his blood again. He spun out of Valko's grip with one of the man's Kimbers in hand. He aimed it into Antoine's face. Steven held the gun less than a few inches from where the eye should be.

"Don't you dare underestimate me, you arrogant bastard," Steven said through gritted teeth. His vision swam and his ear was ringing. He was close enough, however, that none of that would hinder his aim.

Antoine cocked his head, then started laughing. It was a full-on, deep laugh, and it took him a few moments to finish. Antoine said, "Boy, you are a plumb fool. You need fifty-caliber or better to break this armor."

"Or, just enough hits to the weak point you've put in the glass panel on your visor," Steven replied. "I suspect it's bullet resistant, but it's still glass. How accurate are you with that rifle at five yards or less?"

"You're welcome to take that ricochet to the face," Antoine mused.

Valko placed a hand on top of the Kimber, forcing Steven's hand down. "We don't have time for squabbling. If you lose much more blood, today gets a lot worse for you. Keep moving."

Steven handed the pistol back to Valko and stalked away, Antoine's chuckles mocking every labored step. Valko forcibly snatched Steven's arm and supported him. They walked on, Steven and Valko in silence. He forced himself to ignore Antoine's ramblings.

They walked up to a fenced-in lot. There were two gates. One large enough to drive through, and the other sized to walk into the lot. Within the fences topped with concertina wire were long, low buildings. Haven Storage, as promised.

When they got to the gate, Steven pulled his Arsenal-issued ID card from his wallet. It had a gouge in the middle; a claw must have punctured it. He passed it under the scanner and was pleased to hear the machine chime. The walk-in gate swung open with a long squeak.

The path to E-201 was blessedly short. The unit's door was open, revealing a furnished living area. There was a door on either side of the unit. He wondered how much space the safe house took up, considering what all had been housed in this particular room. Much of the group sat on couches set toward the center of the space. A tarp hung from a curved steel rod in the far corner of the unit. Someone cursed in a half-choked sob from behind the tarp. It took a moment for the voice to register in Steven's thoughts as Nyura. Steven guessed Brice would be with her, working to stabilize Pattie.

His mind swam and his vision twisted. The pain had become a dull roar throughout his body, accompanied by a numbness that made it hard to keep moving his feet. Grace cried out and ran forward, reaching out. She pulled up short, as Valko put a hand up.

Curtis stared, slack-jawed and wide-eyed. "Motherf-"

Ladeen slapped him and hissed in his ear, but too loudly. "Enough's enough. Stop being an ass."

Grace reached out again as Valko deposited Steven onto one of the couches. Something pricked his skin, and the cooling sensation of one of Nyura's syringes flooded through him over the course of several tense, silent moments.

Steven watched Valko tour the room, opening the side doors and finally relaxing a little. Antoine stood in the main doorway, watching everyone. Valko let his shotgun rest on its strap and removed his helmet. His eyes were narrowed in concern.

"What was that you injected in him?" asked Valko.

Grace shrugged. "Nyura said to inject him when he got here because his wounds from earlier might have opened in the fighting."

Steven chuckled, and then winced. It still hurt too much. "Hemostatic and painkiller. Unfortunately, I came back with all new wounds. Imagine that."

Mirena crossed her arms, looking at him with a sidelong glance. "Not funny. At least that hasn't changed."

Steven grimaced. "Oh, did I change? Or did you finally look into the eyes of the devil I told you I am?"

Grace's hands went to her hips, eyes narrowing. She practically knelt on the couch next to him, legs tucked under herself. "I want you to stop, Steven. How many times do I have to tell you, you're not who you've said you are?"

He could barely keep his eyes open. "Really? This again? All I've known since I was seven has been danger and death. Kill or die. That's what I am. Knowing you has been pleasant, but it doesn't change anything for me."

Grace reached out, placing a hand on his cheek.

"Yes, this again." She stared into his eyes. "Until you know what I see. Until you see the changes you can make to your own story."

"Well, somebody's getting bold."

She laughed despite herself. Mirena rolled her eyes and turned away.

"You just spent hours risking your life for two people who seem to hate you." She shrugged. "And the rest of us, too. If that doesn't prove my point about you, nothing will."

Antoine raised a hand. "Oh, I hate him, too. He wasn't risking his life for me, though."

Valko turned, eyeing Antoine for a long moment. He turned back around, shaking his head. Valko said, "How are the rest of you?"

Curtis shrugged. "We're alive. Nyura and Brice are in the back there. Pattie took a beating. I don't know how she's doing right now."

Steven's head had cleared some. He could just make out the sounds of Nyura's calm voice. There was relief in that voice. The kind of comfort that came from knowing the worst was over.

He said, "Pattie's going to be fine."

Curtis glared. "And you know this because..."

"Curtis, let me tell you a secret my father told me," Steven said, his head rolling in the other young man's direction. "You have two ears, and one mouth. You should listen twice as much as you speak. Nyura's happy. She saved Pattie. Like I said she would."

Grace turned his face back toward hers. "How is this even possible? How can there be so much doubt, that you can't believe in yourself the way you believe in your friends?"

He smiled at her and found his finger tracing her hair down to her neck. "I do believe in myself, though. Nyura heals. You are grace incarnate. And I'm the reaper, come to devour life. My murdered father's blood was on the knife that cut me down. I'm the warrior his blood molded me into."

Grace smiled back. "Maybe so. But you're more than the warrior. I don't know why you chose to save me and Mirena, but I'm grateful."

"Isn't it obvious?" he asked, eyebrow raised. "You took a chance on me. It's not lost on me that you chose to be my friend, despite my every attempt to keep that from happening."

Her face scrunched. "I did kind of force the issue, huh?"

Mirena scoffed. "Oh, you think? Prancing around your room, singing along to your favorite love songs. All the sneaky little pictures on your phone..."

Grace's face went red. "That's more than enough, Mirena."

Putting a finger to her chin, Mirena looked devious. "Oh, chiquita mala, did I say something I shouldn't have? That's right, he wasn't supposed to know you were practically drooling every time you sighed his name."

Grace shrank into herself. "I...that was..."

Steven put a hand on hers. He smiled and winked. "It's okay. The relief of safety after traumatic stress does weird things to people. Can't trust your own memory, sometimes."

Mirena rolled her eyes and crossed the room to a mini fridge. She opened the refrigerator and pulled a can of soda from it. She opened it and started drinking. She kept stealing glances at Valko's square face.

Valko crossed his arms and shifted, looking around. His gaze seemed to linger a moment or two on Mirena, who turned away quickly to sip her soda, and he hesitated. He shook his head and sighed. It was a strained sound.

From somewhere behind him, Steven made out the sound of the tarp being moved, and footsteps. He looked back. Nyura and Brice emerged and walked over to join the group.

"Didn't know to expect super soldiers," said Nyura. Her torn undershirt was almost soaked through with sweat and blood. "I'd have dressed up a bit more. Welcome to the war, gentlemen."

Antoine snarked. "Ha. ha." He rolled his head to either side and shifted his feet, visibly bored, though he pointedly took a few moments to ogle both Nyura and Mirena.

Valko motioned at Steven. "Steven took a beating. You may want to check him over."

Nyura shook her head. "I swear, I waste my best material with all you serious types. Sheesh!"

She walked around and took in a breath so sharp; it was comparable to the crack of a rifle.

"Well, crap," she said, eyeing Steven. She looked around and started pointing. "I don't have another bed, so I need y'all to make some space. Grace, please scoot so we can lay him down. Brice, get my kit from the back. The rest of you, back the hell out of my light. And somebody tell that asshole at the door to stop staring at my chest, yeah?"

<u>10 Simple Questions</u>

Maurice trudged along, several steps behind Joseph. He sucked in a breath, hating the cold, plastic taste from the filters in his armor, wishing beyond hope to wake up. The only problem being, he knew he wasn't asleep. In his sleep, he could see her. He could never stop thinking about Sybil for long.

Glancing at his databrace, he sighed. The background image of the wrist-mounted computer was a dossier photograph Abaroa had given him. He looked at the sharp cheekbones and hooked nose. The dark hair and soft smile, almost hidden by haunted eyes.

Her voice said, *"It was how fragile I was, wasn't it? That's what attracted you to me. In a way, that's what attracts all broken men to broken women. You finally had someone to protect. You thought you had a say in my future. It gave you reason until you lost me. Now, look at you. Lost because I took away your choice."*

He frowned. *"No. That's not true. You saved me from the Talon. And from Joseph."*

They used to sit on the rooftop of the arsenal. It was a good, quiet place to talk. He missed their conversations. Sybil's mind had intrigued him, she had praised him every time he'd shown her a new gadget. Gave him notes afterward, too.

Joseph turned around. "Wisp, are you with me or what?"

Maurice shook his head, short and sharp. "Yeah, sorry."

"I can't afford for you to be distracted," said Joseph, stepping in close. "Despite how it appears, I can't cover every angle by myself."

"It's hard to lie to yourself, isn't it?" She shook her head, *dark hair cascading. Her smoky mesquite-colored eyes twinkled*

in the starlight. The deep tan of her skin glistened in the fading afternoon sunlight as she sat at the edge of the Arsenal roof. She smiled up at him, using a hand to sweep a portion of hair behind her ear. "It's almost adorable how much you needed my dependence."

Maurice swallowed hard. "I didn't tell you everything about what happened."

Tilting his head, Joseph said softly, "About Fortress?"

"Shit, Cross!" Maurice spat. "Sybil's been dead for two years. You can say her damn name."

In the silence that stretched between them, Maurice took in several deep breaths. His eyes burned with tears, but he couldn't exactly wipe them away through the helmet. He wondered what Joseph would do to him for the outburst, but for some reason, he couldn't bring himself to care about consequences he couldn't predict.

"No, I can't," said Joseph, finally, so softly it startled Maurice. "She earned her callsign, same as you. I will not sully that memory of her while we're on mission. Now, what didn't you tell me?"

"Before she," Maurice trailed off, the words stuck. He cleared his throat. "I just,"

Joseph put a hand on his shoulder, voice surprisingly gentle. "She made a difficult choice. I get that. Is that what's bothering you?"

Maurice put a hand on his helmet, wishing he could press palms into his eyes. "I don't even understand why I'm still on the team. Even Steven had me sorted on sight. I'm a coward. She complained to me about Antoine. I didn't confront him then. I still haven't confronted him, even with what he tried to do to Emily."

Sighing, Joseph said, "Her death is not your fault. And don't you worry about Country Mile."

"Don't worry?" Rage boiled up from Maurice's stomach. "He molested two of our team members and plays devil's advocate against every order you issue."

"Because Karma is a mirror," said Joseph. "And he can't choose targets for shit. He's gotten more than he's given every time he's stepped out of line."

"And Emily?"

"She's away from all this. Most likely safe. In spite of my whining, it looks like it worked out for her."

Maurice's mind settled a little. *In a way, that's true for Sybil, too. Dammit. This is seriously screwed up.*

"Will it ever stop hurting?" Maurice still trembled, even under her touch. Especially under her touch. He couldn't let go.

She shrugged. "Eventually, everything stops. Pain, joy, anger, life, death. It all ends at some point. But...is that why you fight? To avoid an inevitable end? Or are you looking to find one?"

The communications building loomed ahead, a flickering light issuing from a broken door. A Talon stood in the doorway with its back to them. The sight of it breathing in ragged gasps seemed foreboding. It whirled around, snarling.

He returned her touch with shaking fingers, looking into the darkness behind her eyes. "I'm just...so tired. I wasn't ready to lose you."

She embraced him. "If only your love could've saved me. I'd have been immortal."

"Hey, Wisp? Time's up. Wake the hell up and fight!"

Joseph started firing. Talon-types poured from the communications building door on the Arsenal campus. And there was something else, too. Something with red skin. It was smaller than the others, and it was smiling. It moved with inhuman litheness as it slipped behind several Talons.

What the hell is that?

Maurice lifted his rifle and started firing.

<u>11 Necessity</u>

Gusts of wind whipped rain into the hotel window. It almost drowned out the sound of the shower. Emily paced the tiny room over and over, contemplating her next move. The burger hadn't been worth traveling in the opposite direction from the Blue Rock mission. She sighed, flopping down on the plush bed.

Emily closed her eyes, gathering her thoughts, putting various pieces together. Sean didn't listen.

What, exactly, did you expect? You're a literal child, and they've got years of experience. Why the hell would they have actually taken the warnings to heart?

She pressed her lips together, resting a fist on her forehead. People were going to die. A lot of them. She hated not being able to save them. But, as they had reminded her, over and again, they were the adults. They would handle the situation. The sound of the shower stopped.

Emily opened her eyes narrowly.

Don't save them. They've made their choice.

Joseph and the others would be in the heart of danger. And Sean was on his way to complicate said danger much further. Emily almost tensed at the sound of the woman's footsteps padding on the carpet by the other bed. The woman fiddled with a pill bottle, a few moments later swallowing from a bottle of water.

Emily asked, turning to see the female agent. "Hey, Candace. How long would you hold it against me if I got away from you tonight?"

Candace raised an eyebrow. "Considering the disciplinary actions that would be leveled against me? Probably longer than you're thinking. I'd like to be promoted again at some point, after all."

Emily smiled at her. "I could always take you out in your sleep. I am an asparagus, after all."

Candace raised an eyebrow as she wrapped a towel around her wet hair. "The hell is that supposed to mean?"

Emily waved a dismissive hand. "You know. My star sign, or whatever."

"Do you mean an Aquarius?"

Snapping her fingers, Emily said, "Yeah, that."

Candace sighed, pinching the bridge of her nose. "Look, kid, I get it. You're dangerous. Can we not go through this again? We've explained everything ad nauseam, and I'm not your only obstacle in getting away from here."

Shrugging, Emily chuckled. "You said 'obstacle'."

Candace toweled at her hair. "We're taking this seriously. I hope you can see that."

Emily turned back to stare at the ceiling again. "I can see that. I respect it, too. That's why I've been trying to find a way not to have to fight my way out of your custody. I'm going to Blue Rock to help my brother. You and your fellow 'obstacles' are only going to delay me so long."

"Tell me something," said Candace. "About the girl who died. She had a sister named Kathryn, didn't she?"

Emily glanced back at the agent. The woman's emotions still didn't show on her face. Studying her features didn't bring anyone in particular to mind. Candace had warm olive skin, almost creamy in color, and dark brown hair.

"I think that was her name. What of it?"

"Sybil and Kathryn are my nieces. They went missing ten years ago with their father, all presumed dead. When the rumors cropped up about your program, I got hopeful. When I heard Lynn was bringing in a girl they had been able to arrange for, I was hoping it'd be one of them."

The woman I left Blue Rock with. Her name was Lynn. I should remember that.

"For what it's worth, I'm sorry I'm not the girl you were looking for. And for what you've lost."

Candace smiled. "You brought us what we needed to stop them. That's enough for me."

Emily scoffed. "Yeah. Keep thinking that, lady. The Talons and Akuma will change your tune. I hate to say it, but not a single person on that task force has any idea what they're walking into."

"So you've said, multiple times." Candace was mostly dressed now.

Emily took a few deep breaths, emptying her mind and slowing her heart rate. She wiped at dry eyes, hoping for tears she couldn't shed. "I just wish I could help them."

Candace said, "It helps that they don't have to worry about you, too."

I hadn't thought of it that way. The intrusive thought almost broke her forced calm. Emily turned, staring at Agent Candace. A familiar, hollow numbness washed through her.

For all their platitudes, Emily couldn't reasonably rely on these people. For all their efforts, it had taken them ten years to find out the Nomad program even existed. They weren't prepared for the monsters. Or the monstrous things they'd have to do to save whoever was left.

Am I prepared to kill? Joseph always took the reins when it came to that. He never let me go that far. Blackwood probably believed I never had it in me. Emily shook her head, clearing the doubts away. *That man at the diner. I stabbed him.* It was too much to think about at once. Her mission was everything. The only thing.

"A person can only live in a world without heroes for so long," said Emily, pushing up from the bed in a slow, smooth motion. "Before they learn not to look for them."

Candace tilted her head. "Emily? You okay?"

Emily walked forward; eyes locked on Candace. "I'll only ask one more time for you to stand aside."

Candace stepped into a fighting stance. It was a form of martial arts containing elements of Krav Maga, Jeet Kune Do, and Brazilian Jiu-Jitsu. Emily smiled. The stance was good, but Candace's muscle movements would be slowed from having been in the hot water. And even more from the painkiller working its way through her system. The quieter this was, the better it would be. Maybe she could even get a head start.

Yeah, right, dumbass. They've probably got a team listening in on the room. If you're lucky, they haven't started scrambling yet. Get moving. The faster the better.

Emily stepped in and pivoted, spinning past a jab from Candace. The agent's jaw dropped just before Emily slammed an elbow into her gut. As Candace gasped, Emily followed with a hook to the jaw. Candace dropped to the floor, groaning before laying still.

Emily ran to the chair in the corner, snatching the keys from Candace's pants pocket. No gun. Smart of them, but annoying. Emily exited the hotel room and sprinted through the carpeted hallway. The sound of people scrambling out of a room behind her told her everything she needed to know.

She hit the stairwell and rushed deftly down, hopping over the rail to avoid a surprised couple on their way up. She slid the last few feet and hit the push bar on the exterior door, spilling out into the drenched parking lot.

Windswept rain stung her eyes, and a flash of lightning forked across the sky. Rushing to the unmarked black sedan, she pressed the button on the key's remote, unlocking the door. She got in and started the engine, then cursed at herself.

Emily searched around the interior space, wiping uselessly at her eyes with an equally wet arm. The gearbox was easy to find, attached behind the wheel as it was. She pressed down a pedal; nothing happened. She pressed the other and heard the engine's deep growl. Simple enough.

She tried shifting the gearbox. It wouldn't move. She pressed the left pedal and tried again. She put the indicator on the Reverse symbol and pressed the accelerator. The sizable car rocketed back. A group of approaching agents scattered in the car's wake, ducking behind other vehicles.

Suddenly jerked forward, Emily winced. A jolt of pain washed away other sensations, leaving fear in its wake. She'd crunched the sedan into another car. Her heart pounded, and she hoped she knew what she was doing.

"My bad!" she screamed, hysterical laughter bubbling from her throat. "I'm an asparagus!"

She put the car's gearbox to Drive and turned the wheel, pressing the accelerator again. The tires squealed on the pavement and the car jerked around, the tail end sliding into another parked vehicle. The car shot forward through the hotel parking lot.

Glancing off another vehicle, Emily winced. "Oh, yeah. Lights."

Moving a knob, she frowned at the wipers as they started to slap at the rain coming down into the windshield.

"Those too, I suppose," she said to no one in particular. She reached again, twisting another knob next to the vent. Finally, she was rewarded with lights cutting through the dark, slashing rain. She turned the car out onto the roadway.

Emily glanced around at the restaurants to either side of the street, stomach growling. She took the corner a little faster than she intended, the sedan fishtailing through the lane, across the double yellow lines. A car coming through the light behind her blew its horn.

Distant sirens sounded, sending a surge of adrenaline through her. She floored the accelerator.

I need to ditch the G-Ride. Get into an SUV or minivan. Something green or gray. Less noticeable, at the very least.

Expecting the loss of control at the next turn, she prepared for it and cut the wheel right earlier than before. The large sedan squealed, sliding around through the green light in a much smoother motion than before.

She spotted a pizza place to the right and pouted. That was a delicious recent experience and she wished there was time to stop and order one. She focused back on the road ahead. Eating could come after she put some distance between herself and the agents.

An upcoming Walmart sign illuminated the next intersection, right across from an RV sales lot. Emily smiled. She took the turn, stopping at the intersection and slamming the sedan in reverse. She backed it into the RV lot, leaving the lights on and pushing the lever for the turn signal.

Stepping back out into the stormy night, Emily sighed. Lightning crackled through the sky, thunder rumbling not far behind. She sprinted from the lot. Had it not been so late at night, she'd have worried about more traffic.

The narrow street leading to Walmart sported a handful of plazas and fast-food restaurants nearby. She groaned at the distance, slowing to a fast trudge, shoes slipping in the wet grass.

The rain seemed to slacken, and the sound of the sirens was fast approaching. Flashing blue lights brightened the stormy night sky in the distance. She smiled. They'd ignore the sedan for a bit because it looked like it was waiting to turn.

Someone would eventually notice and double back to see why there was a car turning from a closed lot, but every step they took to figure it out would buy her time to get away.

Then again, a lone redhead power-walking uphill in the rain would most certainly be reported...right?

Just in case, Emily cut through the restaurant parking lots. It wouldn't do her any good to be visible from the road when the cops passed by.

Passing behind the last building, the flat facade of the Walmart emerged at the end of a massive stretch of asphalt. Emily dragged her feet a bit, overwhelming intimidation settled in.

Never been in one of these before.

The one thing Emily did know; there were people who would be sympathetic to a teenage girl trying to get home. Or there was the other kind of people. The kind it was better to leave bleeding somewhere. She'd lived with one of those.

Emily didn't have to pretend to be in a bad mood as she walked into the front entrance of the Walmart. She was tired and hungry. The frustration of the entire past week roiled at the surface, welling up inside her throat.

An older black lady working the greeting desk went wide-eyed and put a hand to her mouth. Her name tag read 'Angie'.

"Baby, don't you have an umbrella?" said Angie, voice husky and smooth.

"No," Emily responded. "But listen, I just...need somewhere to dry out for a minute."

The woman came in close and whispered. "Do you need a safe place, honey?"

Emily nodded, knowing from the pressure in her head that her eyes should be a bit red now. Not quite crying red, but close enough, considering she was drenched through from the rain.

Who needs tears when the sky cries for you?

"My boyfriend got a bit crazy," she lied. "I needed some space. He'll probably be looking for me. Him or that dingbat sister of his. I've half a mind to hitchhike to New York or something."

"None of that, now. This ain't the kinda place to be picking up rides from strangers, child. Do I need to call someone for you? The police, or a relative maybe?"

Emily shook her head, hugging herself against the chill setting in from the air conditioner.

"No. I'll be fine. Cops ought to be on their way to the apartment by now, but nothing's going to change."

Angie looked on with a caring, understanding gaze and sniffled, forcing a smile. "Give me a moment, then we can at least get you some coffee."

Angie waved over a person with a yellow vest to take over her spot. She walked Emily to the back of the store, through an employee's-only double door. They went past a couple of small offices, and into a large cinder-block room filled with posters about the legal rights of employees. And one about how to lift boxes.

The Walmart break room held heavy notes of stale coffee and burned popcorn. There was a sink, two restroom doors, and a coffee pot. Three different drink vending machines. Five plastic picnic tables surrounded by folding metal chairs were spaced evenly throughout the room.

An older man sipped at a cup of coffee, eyeing the two of them as they walked in. At a glare from Angie, he averted his gaze. Emily thanked her, slipping into the women's restroom.

Emily dried herself the best she could with paper towels, contemplating her next move. She had to keep moving or risk being found. More than that, she had to make sure she'd be going in the right direction.

Without money, a weapon, a vehicle, or a map, Emily stared at her haggard face in the mirror. She really was a sight, wasn't she? Pale, freckled face with red-rimmed emerald eyes and sopping, tangled copper strands of hair. A right mess.

"Priority one," she whispered to her face in the mirror. "Look human again. You won't get very far with anyone looking like a zombie."

She stacked a few paper towels together and used them to pat her hair as dry as she could manage. She pulled her fingers through it, and, pleased as she could be, took a hair tie from her pocket and put it in a ponytail.

Emily washed her face in the sink, then dried it and tested a smile. Still kind of a crooked nose and too-large eyes, but there was only so much she cared to do about that.

Sighing, Emily's smile faltered. "It's a shame I can't blend in like Sean, huh?"

She walked out of the restroom. Angie was there, fiddling with the coffee pot. She turned to rummage in a cabinet and came back with a plastic spoon and a styrofoam cup. The fresh coffee percolating in the brewer let off a pungent, nutty aroma. A definite far cry from the caustic bouquet of whatever had been brewed before.

Angie smiled sweetly and pulled a chair out from a table. Emily shrank in the chair at the prickle in her chest. The lies had begun to blossom into needles of guilt. It couldn't be helped if she were to stay ahead of the agents, but it still sucked. Emily forced herself to feel numb to the lies and returned a halfhearted smile of her own.

"Don't you worry, child," said Angie, stirring the cup with a spoon. "This is my own coffee from home. Not that tar *these* heathens be drinking."

The man at the other table snorted a laugh. "It's coffee, Angie. It's not supposed to taste *good*."

Angie grinned at him. "You're still old, ain't you? I ain't drinking dirt till I'm dead."

The man tilted his cup in mock salute, his laugh boisterous and unrestrained. Angie set down the steaming cup of coffee the color of natural brown sugar and turned to start filling another.

Emily picked up the cup, blowing at the edge, enjoying the soft play of steam washing back up toward her face. She took a sip. It wasn't as bitter as she'd expected. It tasted of a wonderful blend of caramel, vanilla, wood smoke, and almonds, and had a sweet, earthy finish. She stared at the cup, eyes wide.

"I know," said Angie. "It's good, huh? Jack Daniels-brand coffee with a dash of almond milk."

Emily's eyes went wide.

Angie laughed, "It ain't alcohol, girl. Good lord."

She walked back over to the coffee maker and reached into a cabinet, coming back with a black canister with the branding on it.

Angie said, "They coat the beans in their whiskey before they roast 'em. Cooking it evaporates the alcohol and leaves the flavor."

"It's delicious," said Emily. "I'll have to remember that. Thank you."

Angie sat down next to Emily, sipping from her own cup. After a few minutes, the man got up and grumbled about getting back to work and left the break room. It dawned on Emily that she was alone with Angie now.

"I-" Emily hesitated; the words stuck in her throat. *How can I explain it? Lying to assholes is easy. Lying to nice ladies with coffee sucks!*

"I don't really know nothing about your situation, honey," said Angie finally, sucking on her teeth. She sighed after a soft, quiet moment, "And the good Lord knows I don't need to. Got enough goin' on with my own babies."

Emily sat there, staring into the coffee like it was a wishing well. Like she could drop in a silver coin, and change her life. Be Angie's child, instead of a weapon. This sweet woman just didn't know how right she was. Emily swallowed the lump forming in her throat, taking another long sip of coffee to try washing the sour taste of guilt and fear down for good. If she focused hard enough, she could still pick out the bitter taste of the roasted beans.

Angie sighed. "But I know what it looks like when a girl is in trouble. I tell you, child. Looks to me like you stepped in a great big pile of shit. Walkin' round in a storm, 'bout to catch your death."

"I wish I could tell you everything," Emily admitted quietly. She ignored the surprised flutter of her heart at the admission. "But you're right."

Angie was looking at her sidelong. Emily took in several deep breaths, pushing the emotion back down again and again. Her eyes started to ache with the effort.

Emily looked at her. "I have to keep moving. I'm in very real danger. The kind the police can't help with before it's too late. I just need to get out of town."

"How far you need to get?"

"I'm trying to get back home to Arkansas," said Emily, folding her hands together in her lap. "I have a brother there. He's all the family I have, and he probably hates me for leaving. I should never have left with Sean."

Angie frowned. "That's a long way from here. How old are you, girl?"

"Eighteen," she lied again.

Angie nodded, resolute. "Wait here, baby. I'll be right back."

Emily drank the rest of the coffee in her cup while she waited. Less than ten minutes passed, and Angie returned, carrying a small envelope and a checkout bag.

"It ain't much," she said, proffering the envelope. "But I hope it helps you get where you're going."

Emily's face heated now, the emotion impossible to contain. Blinking, the tear escaped without her consent.

"Thank you," she choked. "How do I pay you back when I get to my brother?"

Angie held Emily's hands in her own. They were warm and gentle but also firm and calloused.

Angie smiled. "Don't you worry about that, baby. All you gotta do for me, is when you find yourself in a place to help someone else, do it. World's got enough hate and violence in it that it can afford a few of us to be good to people."

Emily smiled through teary eyes and leaned into embracing Angie. *How can such a good person exist in this world?* Knowing what she'd likely have to do, Emily stayed silent and rested her head against the woman's shoulder.

When Emily drew away, Angie excused herself to the restroom. Emily thanked her again and walked back out to the sales floor. Looking in the envelope, she found three hundred dollars. Emily sighed in frustration. She could only hope to one day be able to do as Angie had told her.

It only took a few minutes for Emily to pick up the things she felt would be necessary. A road atlas and a pre-made sandwich definitely made the list.

As she left the store, the air was still moist and puddles stood sentry. However, the storm had passed. Looking past the fast-food restaurants, she saw the government sedan. Agents milled around the car. Some appeared to be searching the vehicle. One agent stood near the intersection and watched the road in either direction.

Emily groaned and adjusted the ball cap now concealing her red locks. *All right; it's now or never.* She walked purposefully across the parking lot, fixing on a likely vehicle: an older model Honda. She glanced about to be sure no one was looking at her, before getting to work. It took a little under two minutes to swap the plates with a nearby car, manipulate the door open with a screwdriver and a manual blood-pressure cuff, and hotwire the car. As the Honda came to life, she thought of Nikifor and smiled.

"Ugh, Spock," she said to the empty car, closing her eyes in relief. "I hate that you were right all along. Apparently, I did need to know this."

She took a moment to familiarize herself with the controls before pulling away through the lot. Circling around to the back of the lot, she eased out onto a side street. Two stoplights later she merged onto the highway.

This late at night, she'd be able to make decent time. Based on the route she'd determined using the atlas before leaving the store, she had a roughly eight to nine-hour drive ahead of her. It made her groan again, knowing she had so long to go until she arrived at Blue Rock. A situation could change from life to death in seconds and she was still hours away from even knowing if there was anyone left who needed her.

12 The Scars Abound

Steven's gut stung like it had been held over a fire for hours with the flames just licking his skin. He opened his eyes and then winced, feeling a pinch.

"Stop squirming, dammit!" said Nyura, tense. "I'm almost done with your stitches."

Someone scoffed. "Yo, Proximity. You good now? We've been here a solid thirty minutes. We've still got things to do."

Valko said, "Yeah. Nyura, once you guys are rested enough, make your way to the Arsenal. We'll be housing survivors on base until we can finish sweeping the city."

Steven reached out on instinct, snagging Valko's wrist. "Who ordered us back there?"

Nyura cursed and grumbled at Steven with a scathing one-eyed glare. "Stop. Moving."

"Cross," said Valko. "He figured it would be a good, central spot that we could defend easier. Plus, the private rooms will go a long way to help calm people."

Steven let go of the wrist, taking more care not to shift so much this time. "Harper said something about the Arsenal. About how this started there. It had something to do with someone named Richards, but I don't understand."

Valko narrowed his eyes. "Osric Richards is the head researcher in the labs. He worked with Blackwood directly on most of our tech. Harper was only there on the weekends. But what could they have to do with this?"

Steven said, "This is apparently a virus. And, somehow or another, it's his. I don't know how Harper's connected. As far as I knew, he was just a chemistry teacher with a penchant for philosophy."

Valko raised an eyebrow, a fitting enough invitation for Steven to continue.

"All I'm saying," said Steven, grunting through an insert of the needle. "We can't trust the people in charge at the Arsenal. There's too much they haven't told us. Too many things that don't add up."

Valko smiled. "Shut it, puke. No reason to scare your friends with your inane theory. Hell, you're starting to sound like my brother."

Steven raised an eyebrow. *Holy hell, he's bad at covering his lies.*

Valko chuckled. "Your concerns are valid enough. Niki said some similar stuff earlier. This place is secure enough for you and your friends to bunker here until this blows over."

Antoine huffed. "Oh, so now it's okay to ignore our orders. Cause one little pissant has a bad feeling?"

Glaring at Antoine, Valko trembled. "The orders are to extract survivors *as needed*. Quite clearly, this group doesn't need it."

Antoine shook his head and blew out a breath.

Valko donned his helmet, snapping it into place. He checked over his shotgun again and walked out, Antoine trailing him into the deepening shadows of early evening.

Nyura pulled the last stitch tight and cut the thread. She blotted the area gently with a cloth and applied a large square bandage. She sat back on the arm of the couch and sighed, wiping an arm across her forehead.

Steven groaned. His head continued to throb, and his right ear still rang. Tilting his head back, he spotted Grace watching over him from the other nearby chair.

"So, there we are," said Nyura. "Everyone's been seen to. Pattie should be out a while longer."

Steven turned back to her. "I think you're safer here than at the Arsenal. Something very screwed up happened there, and I need to know what before I'll trust Grace to it."

Grace said, "So, you're still going?"

"After we secure your parents, yes. I need to know what the hell those bastards did to this city."

Nyura walked over to a trash can, where she stripped the gloves, she'd been using and tossed them in. "What if," she said, hesitating, "they're not your answers to uncover?"

Narrowing his eyes, Steven glared. "What's that supposed to mean?"

Nyura looked at him pointedly. "No disrespect, but you already have a mission, sir. Get us the hell out of this alive. Screw the secrets in that death trap. I agree that we're safer here. I don't agree that there's anything worth knowing there."

"I shot Harper no fewer than three times." Steven's hand shook, and he pressed it into his lap to steady it. "Every single time, it should have been a kill shot. Twice in the chest by the heart. Once in the head."

Shrugging, Nyura crossed her arms. "And?"

Steven fought the frustration, but it forced its way out anyway. "And not only did he recover from every single one of those kill shots in a matter of minutes, he came back twice and nearly killed me both times. If the people in charge of us got away with creating something like that, can you imagine what else they've done?"

Nyura shuddered. Steven watched widening eyes around the room as the implication took hold.

"I can't believe I'm saying this," said Curtis, crossing his arms, "but you have a solid point."

Steven started. "When did you start agreeing with me?"

He groaned, forcing himself to sit up. His head pounded and his gut seized in pain.

Steven gritted his teeth and tried to maneuver his body upright.

Grace placed gentle hands on his chest. "Stop. You'll pop your stitches!"

Nyura glared. "Don't you dare! You ruin my work, and I'll find something no one could ever think was lethal to stab you with!"

Steven sighed, "I'll be fine. It's not like I'm going for a run."

Grace moved her hands away quickly, like she'd touched a hot stovetop. The number of people glaring at his movement caused him to pause and roll his eyes before finding his words again. "Nothing I find there will be good. More than likely, I won't even make it back out. But if this is going to end--and I mean, really end--then we need whatever secrets we can find there."

Nyura frowned, her eye going hard and glassy. "Let the guys with armor find the secrets. You're barely moving as it is."

Steven reached out and gathered her into a hug. Hot tears tickled his shoulder as she squeezed back, harder than was comfortable. Steven breathed through the pain. Nyura pulled away from him and wiped her eye before dropping her hands with an agonized groan.

"I get it," he said.

"No the hell you don't!" she cried. "That's the problem. You think you know, but you don't."

Steven sat there, stunned by the words. Exhaustion seeped in between pulses of pain.

Curtis sneered. "How can you expect a machine to understand what we're going through emotionally?"

Nyura whispered, "That's not what I'm saying at all."

Steven's arms stiffened. He forced himself to stand. His vision faded into bright spots for too long. Everything hurt. Inside and out.

"Is that why you hate me, Curtis?" he whispered, smiling sardonically. "It's more refreshing than you'd think to know someone sees the monster within."

Curtis' face seemed to shrink. He hugged himself and swallowed hard.

"Please, stop!" Grace sobbed. She stood, pointing a finger. "I don't care why he hates you! You're a good person, dammit!"

Steven turned at the sound of someone choking. Mirena spat and coughed a few times, holding a hand up.

"Sorry," spluttered Mirena. She recovered her composure. 'I've been trying to get Grace to accidentally cuss for over a year. Kind of a weak one, but I guess that gets you a point."

Curtis shrugged as rubbed an arm across his forehead. "Look. We've never been friends. But I've been a total ass today. For what it's worth, I'm sorry."

"Somebody find me a new Curtis," Steven said, looking with a strained smile. "This one's broken."

Curtis hung his head and turned away with a chuckle.

Steven pressed his hands to his eyes. The heat within his face was unbearable. His pulse beat right there behind his eyes. It still felt too weak. He swayed, hating the quiver of his lip. Someone grabbed him. Steadied him.

"Stop," said Grace in his ear. "Please, stop being so mean to yourself."

"Can you honestly say you're not afraid of me?" Steven choked out.

"You haven't tried to hurt me," she said. "Why should I be afraid?"

She squeezed, breaking through the harsh feelings that had bubbled up through him. He sagged into her embrace, releasing a slow breath. He wondered, for a moment. The peace that washed over him bypassed his understanding, and clenched muscles loosened. Relief welled up, spilling out through his eyes.

Without meaning to, he returned her embrace. Her golden hair smelled earthy and floral, but with a subtle hint of motor oil. He wondered at that until he felt her trembling. She gave a short sniffle, then stepped back with a strange grimace on her face.

He smiled. "Did I mess up the hug? Can't imagine I'd be any good at it."

Grace rubbed at her eyes with a sad-sounding chuckle. "No, it's not that." She hesitated, placing a hand on his chest. "You kind of smell...really bad."

Steven grimaced, lifting an arm. Testing the scent, even through his now stuffy nose, he found she was right." Okay, so," he said, trailing off a moment. "Wet puppy dipped in kerosene and covered in dirty nickels is a turn-off. Got it."

A chorus of snorted laughter around the room made Steven grin. There was even a little bit of snickering coming from behind the curtain at the back of the room. At the sound, Nyura turned expectantly and hopped over the back of the couch, half sprinting to the closed-off space.

Mirena threw her can in a trash bin and glared at him, a playful look on her face." Ay pendejo," she said, wiping at her chin with a relatively clean part of her shirt. "You made me laugh soda into my nose twice now. That shit hurts, cabron."

Steven tilted his head, grinning through the pain. He quipped, "How do you suck at cursing in two languages, though?"

She pointed a finger at him like a knife. "You're lucky I don't still have that can, or I'd throw it at your smug face."

13 Simple Answers

Nikifor crept along the street, keenly aware of the disadvantages of being alone. He moved with long strides, swiveling every few feet to keep his surroundings in view. At least two Talons stalked behind him, so he picked up his pace just a pinch.

He watched the readout in his helmet's heads-up display as well, waiting for the signal to be restored. Being able to communicate with the rest of the team would go a long way to making him feel better about the situation. There was only so far intuition could get a person.

Rounding a corner, he pressed a device into the alley wall behind him. Moments later, the device popped and the Talons screamed in surprise. Nikifor turned back around the corner and popped two shots into each face. They slumped in the wire trap without another sound.

The streets around him settled back into the sound of flames on the wind. Shoes scuffed on the pavement across the street, and he turned. A group of ten people ran, some stumbling, three Talons in pursuit. Nikifor lifted his rifle, firing into one of the Talon's shins.

The group veered, and someone ran toward his line of fire. Nikifor sucked at his teeth and cursed. He ran forward and bounded onto the bed of a damaged pickup truck. He placed several more shots, finishing the three Talons.

He lowered his rifle and glanced about, then approached the group. They had stopped at a respectable distance, many of them leaning on nearby cars for support. One person sat, sagging on the ground, rocking back and forth.

One of the adults raised a hand. He held a pump-action shotgun in his other hand. He was an older man in his forties, with a round, wise face and shattered glasses.

He lifted the shotgun level with Nikifor's head. "Who are you, and what do you want?"

Lowering his rifle, Nikifor stood at rest. "Specialist Nikifor Stoyan, Nomad Task Group. I'm currently on mission to protect and escort civilians to safety."

The man jerked his chin at Nikifor. "What's with the space suit, son?"

Nikifor shrugged and said, "It's an experimental armor platform, resistant to small arms fire and bladed weapons. Anything more is classified. Also, I wasn't paying attention during the briefing."

He's still frowning. Tough crowd, I guess. Any of the guys would have found that hilarious.

"So, you're from that military base?" he said carefully, lowering the shotgun.

"Yeah. There are only a few of us. We're doing what we can to get a handle on things." Nikifor looked over the group. "Has anyone been injured?"

The man pointed out three people who were wounded. Two of them had superficial wounds. The last one, however. The young man who had been rocking on the ground was pale with hollow eyes, a large gash in one arm. His lips were almost blue, and he was breathing fast.

A woman knelt and spoke in a calm, firm voice to the young man, but he didn't respond except to try backing away from her. He looked so weak, but his eyes darted around unconstrained.

She called over her shoulder. "Could I get some help restraining him, so I can get the bandage set? He's lost a lot of blood."

Nikifor let the rifle rest on its strap then moved to pin the young man's arms. The woman worked efficiently, sterilizing and dressing the wound. The young man still struggled, unfocused and afraid.

"I ain't scared of you, metal man!" said the wounded young man piteously, pinned as he was.

The woman finished wrapping the wound and looked up through bleary eyes. She nodded, and Nikifor released the young man, who went back to hugging his own knees. The woman leaned back into the arms of the man with the shotgun.

Nikifor grunted. "There's a safe place nearby. Follow me."

The man with the shotgun looked pointedly at him. "I'm getting these people to that military base. Then I need to find my girls."

Nikifor raised an eyebrow, though he knew the man couldn't see it. This man was not a trained fighter. His stance was wrong. He wasn't being watchful enough. "Are you any good with that Remington?"

The man looked down. "Well, I haven't shot anything yet."

"Any particular reason you're carrying a weapon you don't intend to fire?"

"Son, we don't have time for you to stand there and judge me. I bought the damn thing to scare punk kids away from breaking into my house. I wasn't getting ready to fight monsters."

"Then listen to me and follow. This kid won't make it to the Arsenal. He's already in shock. Just back down this alley is a safe-looking place. Maybe I can help him there."

The man looked at the woman and she nodded, face pinched.

"Okay," said the man, hefting the shotgun. "We'll follow you."

Nikifor nodded and turned on his heel, raising his rifle to the ready position. He led the group of survivors in silence. Their fearful whispers bolstered his resolve.

The fact I'm not scared at all should make me concerned. What the hell am I, that this isn't affecting me?

He responded to a nearby sound by aiming his rifle sights. He caught a glimpse of dark metal. The figure waved. Approaching, Nikifor stopped next to Valko and Antoine.

"That other group still here?" he asked.

"Yeah. I see you have wounded. Nyura's in the safehouse."

"Alright. This group is getting rather large. After we get the wounded treated, we should move everyone to the Arsenal and reset."

"About that," said Valko. He filled Nikifor in on Steven's report of Dr. Harper.

"There's so much more to this than we thought," said Nikifor. "If I remember right, Harper was there when we got tested against the Akuma."

"Well, that sucks," said Valko. "Let's get in there and make a plan. I wonder if Steven will be happy to be right."

Antoine chuckled. "That puke? He ain't never happy."

Nikifor and the group of survivors followed the other two Nomads through the alley to the storage unit. Nikifor smiled behind his helmet at the sight. With this many able-bodied fighters, they really could make this spot defensible. It was almost too good to be true.

The man with the shotgun and the woman in the group ran forward, embracing two of the girls. The other survivors filtered around the room, and Ladeen and Brice went around offering snacks and drinks. Ladeen and one of the other survivors escorted the boy in shock to Nyura's cordoned off area.

Steven stood, arms crossed, brows furrowed toward the deepening dusk behind Nikifor.

"Valko told me what's bothering you," said Nikifor. "I hate to say it, but you're right to be worried."

Steven cut his eyes at Nikifor. "Then this short respite might not mean anything to our survival."

"Afraid not. At least, not unless we can get some reinforcements, and possibly a way to stop this."

Steven rubbed at his face and sighed. The scars on his body seemed to crinkle with the tensing of his chest muscles. His sigh burbled into a groan.

"Why does it keep getting worse," he said finally.

Nikifor removed his helmet, smiling. "Don't panic now. One way or the other, we're nearing the end of this thing."

The man with the shotgun looked at Nikifor, incredulous. "How old are you?"

Nikifor said, "Does that matter right now?"

Shaking his head, the man raised his hands. "Look, I'm not sure about putting our lives in the hands of a bunch of kids playing war."

Nyura tore from behind the curtain, glaring. All the newcomers stood transfixed at her deep frown and unkempt appearance. *She is quite the sight. One eyed and covered in blood. Like one of those post-apocalyptic heroines from the novels Emily likes to read.* Brice moved to stand between them as the man turned to look at her.

glared. "I thought we agreed that was in the bad
ory?"
, Nikifor snapped. "We don't have the advantage you
ve. No fence, lots of gunfire to attract hostiles, and
e not fit to run. And yes, you're included in that."
said, "Right now, we have the benefit of being in an
position. They have to come to us. We should get
d Brice on the roof, and hold here. Two snipers gives
verage for us to fight back."
uch extra ammunition did you bring? We've got at
quads, and who knows how many Talons are on the

waved absently at the other room. "There's plenty
we're quick about punching through, we shouldn't
ry about it."
pointed up toward the roof. "If the enemy has sniper
oyed, we're outflanked."
g, Steven's eyes flashed dark thoughts. "Unless
ing anti-materiel rifles like Antoine, you guys
ne. We can keep you covered from ground level."
nly one sniper can be on the roof. And we still end
euvered. I like how you're thinking," said Nikifor,
eally do. But you need to assume the enemy is
They came to us, and they're not going to wait for
it all out. Right now, the priority needs to be
civilians and wounded out of harm's way."
hissed. "That's the whole damn point I'm making.
emy into this kill box, instead of driving us into
e."

Nyura's voice was dangerously cold as she strained against
Brice's hold. "Excuse the hell out of me, but maybe I missed the
part where any of this looked fun to you!"

Brice whispered to her.

"Hell out of my way, Brice." Nyura snapped at him. Brice
shook his head.

Nikifor nodded his head to her. "The wounded need you
more, ma'am."

Nyura's glare shifted to Nikifor's face. She glowered at him
with a red-rimmed, gray eye. Several pale trails cut through the
muck on one side of her face. On the other was a soiled patch.

Steven turned to face the man. He spoke softly. "No
disrespect, sir. But if that's how you feel, the door is right there.
Nobody's keeping you prisoner."

The blonde girl put a hand on the man's elbow. "Dad, stop.
They're good people. And, more importantly, they're keeping us
safe."

The shock pulsed through, but Steven held still, his need to
see Grace out of danger outweighing all else at the moment.

"I just-" the man stammered.

"I get it," said Nikifor, glowering. "This is the kind of
situation we're supposed to be able to look to adults to fix for
us. We don't have that luxury."

Steven turned back. "Okay. So, no need to get Grace and
Mirena home, since Grace's parents are here. Next step, we
need to secure this spot and get to the bottom of whatever the
hell happened at the Arsenal."

Antoine chimed in, "Gotta get there first, dipstick."

"Anything you'd like to share, Antoine?" said Steven.

Yawning, Antoine said, "Yeah. We're about to have armed
company."

Valko turned. "Is it backup? Another SOU squad?"

"Nah, looks like base security, but wrong. Not sure I know these guys. They're driving a black SUV, so they fit the movie bad-guy stereotype. All black body armor, yep. Some sorta knife emblem on the shoulder. That looks familiar." Something slapped into Antoine's helmet with a crack. He shook his head and moved back inside the door. "Oh? They want to play!"

The late evening came alive with the sound of gunfire. Rounds splashed across the concrete outside.

Antoine leaned out the door, standing against several bullets that smashed into his armor and pulled the trigger. His rifle exploded with sound, causing the entire group to flinch.

Steven glanced around the room. "Everybody that isn't fighting, get down and stay down. Nikifor and Brice, give Antoine some cover so he can get to a better vantage. Valko, you're on close security. Brice, you got a rifle yet?"

"On the way, sir." Brice ran from the attached room, carrying several weapons. He handed Steven a pistol and several magazines.

Steven's calm commands were refreshing, but he was thinking small. They needed to gain the advantage. Nikifor smiled to himself as he put his helmet back on.

"Hey," said Nikifor, pulling a small black orb from his pocket. "One small addendum."

He could almost see the amusement cross Antoine's face as he looked at the object. Wisp had designed these for him. Programmable smart grenades with legs, so they could be deployed in a variety of situations. One hundred and eighty grams of stable plastic explosive goodness inside a walking steel shell. Wisp had called them by their model and revision

---

numbers, but Nikifor felt 'Spider bom[...] just so.

Antoine turned away and took an[...]

Nikifor ran out from behind Anto[...] crashing through the fence, armored[...] side, firing AK-47 rifles their way. He[...] pressed a button on his wrist-mount[...]

The spinning spider bomb lande[...] of the speeding vehicle. It rolled only[...] sprouted eight mechanical legs and [...] underneath and detonated, spraying[...] the vehicle. The soldiers who had bee[...] rolled and leaped to their feet, movin[...] building for cover, firing as they mov[...] the fact his right arm hung limply, dr[...]

Nikifor counted five. The driver h[...] flaming wreckage. There was anothe[...] the right. Possibly a second squad, m[...] twelve guys with guns. Talons shriek[...] noise was attracting them. Somethin[...] bothered him. Their movements seer[...] Almost simultaneous.

Antoine turned to him. "Well? Do[...] this."

Nikifor moved to Steven and Nyu[...] strategy. Think you two can handle th[...]

Nyura nodded. "There's a pair of a[...] use, but we'll need a hole."

Nikifor replied, "Leave that to us.[...] Arsenal."

A sound chimed in Nikifor's helmet, and he let himself be distracted by the orange bar, indicating a radio connection. The speaker in his helmet crackled softly.

"This is Wisp, does anyone hear me?"

"Yeah," said Nikifor, holding up a hand. "We hear you. Good news, right?"

"The hell is all that noise, Web?" Joseph's voice.

"We're taking accurate fire from an unidentified group of commandos who might be on something. At least one of them has a severely lacerated arm, and they're pressing in hard."

Wisp spoke. "I've got you guys positioned in the Eighth Street Safehouse. There should be an entrance to the sewer in that building, under the motor pool, with a straight shot east to the Arsenal parking lot."

Nikifor said, "Well, that's very good news. The safe house is compromised." He turned to the others, relaying the information.

Steven grinned. "I like option three. I already smell like shit."

"Okay, get these people there, Steven. You and Valko run point. I'll trap the doors and lead the commandos in another direction."

Steven's smile fell into a grimace. "You're going to run interference by yourself?"

Nikifor tried to ignore the way his heart changed rhythm at Steven's words. *I really don't have good odds, armor be damned. It's good he can't see my face right now. Might try to talk me out of it.*

"Yeah, they'll probably surround me." Nikifor forced the chuckle. "Poor bastards."

Steven's sardonic grin betrayed too much understanding as he laughed along, clapping Nikifor's shoulder plate with his free hand. He nodded to Nikifor and turned on his heel, gathering everyone into a somewhat loose grouping, relaying whispered orders. Grace's father moved reluctantly, but he stayed quiet and listened as Steven organized their retreat.

Antoine took another shot and retreated into the unit, and the group went through the far door to where the armored vehicles would be sitting. Nikifor placed two of the wire trap devices on either side of the open bay and activated their proximity triggers, then moved through the far door himself. Just before he closed it, he set down another spider bomb.

He gave it a command. Its legs sprouted, and it scurried underneath the couch, where it stood still. He input a quick command, linking the spider bomb to the wire traps and a sensor in his armor. As soon as the squad breached, he'd need to be moving.

He let the door click closed behind him and turned. Valko hauled at the manhole cover, the steel scraping across the concrete. When it opened, he stood and took Pattie from Nyura, using one arm to hold her as he descended the ladder.

Showoff...

Nikifor smiled, turning his attention back to the door behind him. Several tense moments progressed as the group filtered into the sewers. The wire traps sent a signal to his heads-up display. They had snapped shut. Five seconds later, the spider bomb's explosion tumbled through the building.

The garage door of the unit exploded inward. Someone screamed. Nikifor turned back. The kid who had been nursing an arm lay motionless, a shard of serrated metal embedded in his lower back.

Nyura's voice was dangerously cold as she strained against Brice's hold. "Excuse the hell out of me, but maybe I missed the part where any of this looked fun to you!"

Brice whispered to her.

"Hell out of my way, Brice." Nyura snapped at him. Brice shook his head.

Nikifor nodded his head to her. "The wounded need you more, ma'am."

Nyura's glare shifted to Nikifor's face. She glowered at him with a red-rimmed, gray eye. Several pale trails cut through the muck on one side of her face. On the other was a soiled patch.

Steven turned to face the man. He spoke softly. "No disrespect, sir. But if that's how you feel, the door is right there. Nobody's keeping you prisoner."

The blonde girl put a hand on the man's elbow. "Dad, stop. They're good people. And, more importantly, they're keeping us safe."

The shock pulsed through, but Steven held still, his need to see Grace out of danger outweighing all else at the moment.

"I just-" the man stammered.

"I get it," said Nikifor, glowering. "This is the kind of situation we're supposed to be able to look to adults to fix for us. We don't have that luxury."

Steven turned back. "Okay. So, no need to get Grace and Mirena home, since Grace's parents are here. Next step, we need to secure this spot and get to the bottom of whatever the hell happened at the Arsenal."

Antoine chimed in, "Gotta get there first, dipstick."

"Anything you'd like to share, Antoine?" said Steven.

Yawning, Antoine said, "Yeah. We're about to have armed company."

Valko turned. "Is it backup? Another SOU squad?"

"Nah, looks like base security, but wrong. Not sure I know these guys. They're driving a black SUV, so they fit the movie bad-guy stereotype. All black body armor, yep. Some sorta knife emblem on the shoulder. That looks familiar." Something slapped into Antoine's helmet with a crack. He shook his head and moved back inside the door. "Oh? They want to play!"

The late evening came alive with the sound of gunfire. Rounds splashed across the concrete outside.

Antoine leaned out the door, standing against several bullets that smashed into his armor and pulled the trigger. His rifle exploded with sound, causing the entire group to flinch.

Steven glanced around the room. "Everybody that isn't fighting, get down and stay down. Nikifor and Brice, give Antoine some cover so he can get to a better vantage. Valko, you're on close security. Brice, you got a rifle yet?"

"On the way, sir." Brice ran from the attached room, carrying several weapons. He handed Steven a pistol and several magazines.

Steven's calm commands were refreshing, but he was thinking small. They needed to gain the advantage. Nikifor smiled to himself as he put his helmet back on.

"Hey," said Nikifor, pulling a small black orb from his pocket. "One small addendum."

He could almost see the amusement cross Antoine's face as he looked at the object. Wisp had designed these for him. Programmable smart grenades with legs, so they could be deployed in a variety of situations. One hundred and eighty grams of stable plastic explosive goodness inside a walking steel shell. Wisp had called them by their model and revision

Steven's sardonic grin betrayed too much understanding as he laughed along, clapping Nikifor's shoulder plate with his free hand. He nodded to Nikifor and turned on his heel, gathering everyone into a somewhat loose grouping, relaying whispered orders. Grace's father moved reluctantly, but he stayed quiet and listened as Steven organized their retreat.

Antoine took another shot and retreated into the unit, and the group went through the far door to where the armored vehicles would be sitting. Nikifor placed two of the wire trap devices on either side of the open bay and activated their proximity triggers, then moved through the far door himself. Just before he closed it, he set down another spider bomb.

He gave it a command. Its legs sprouted, and it scurried underneath the couch, where it stood still. He input a quick command, linking the spider bomb to the wire traps and a sensor in his armor. As soon as the squad breached, he'd need to be moving.

He let the door click closed behind him and turned. Valko hauled at the manhole cover, the steel scraping across the concrete. When it opened, he stood and took Pattie from Nyura, using one arm to hold her as he descended the ladder.

Showoff…

Nikifor smiled, turning his attention back to the door behind him. Several tense moments progressed as the group filtered into the sewers. The wire traps sent a signal to his heads-up display. They had snapped shut. Five seconds later, the spider bomb's explosion tumbled through the building.

The garage door of the unit exploded inward. Someone screamed. Nikifor turned back. The kid who had been nursing an arm lay motionless, a shard of serrated metal embedded in his lower back.

A sound chimed in Nikifor's helmet, and he let himself be distracted by the orange bar, indicating a radio connection. The speaker in his helmet crackled softly.

"This is Wisp, does anyone hear me?"

"Yeah," said Nikifor, holding up a hand. "We hear you. Good news, right?"

"The hell is all that noise, Web?" Joseph's voice.

"We're taking accurate fire from an unidentified group of commandos who might be on something. At least one of them has a severely lacerated arm, and they're pressing in hard."

Wisp spoke. "I've got you guys positioned in the Eighth Street Safehouse. There should be an entrance to the sewer in that building, under the motor pool, with a straight shot east to the Arsenal parking lot."

Nikifor said, "Well, that's very good news. The safe house is compromised." He turned to the others, relaying the information.

Steven grinned. "I like option three. I already smell like shit."

"Okay, get these people there, Steven. You and Valko run point. I'll trap the doors and lead the commandos in another direction."

Steven's smile fell into a grimace. "You're going to run interference by yourself?"

Nikifor tried to ignore the way his heart changed rhythm at Steven's words. *I really don't have good odds, armor be damned. It's good he can't see my face right now. Might try to talk me out of it.*

"Yeah, they'll probably surround me." Nikifor forced the chuckle. "Poor bastards."

numbers, but Nikifor felt 'Spider bombs' rolled off the tongue just so.

Antoine turned away and took another shot. "Hell yeah, do it..."

Nikifor ran out from behind Antoine and saw the SUV crashing through the fence, armored soldiers hanging on the side, firing AK-47 rifles their way. He hurled the orb and pressed a button on his wrist-mounted databrace.

The spinning spider bomb landed on the ground just ahead of the speeding vehicle. It rolled only a moment before it sprouted eight mechanical legs and ran forward. It scurried underneath and detonated, spraying shrapnel and flames into the vehicle. The soldiers who had been hanging from the sides rolled and leaped to their feet, moving behind the edges of the building for cover, firing as they moved. One of them ignored the fact his right arm hung limply, dripping blood.

Nikifor counted five. The driver hadn't made it out of the flaming wreckage. There was another crash from somewhere to the right. Possibly a second squad, making at least ten or twelve guys with guns. Talons shrieked in the darkness. The noise was attracting them. Something about the commandos bothered him. Their movements seemed too much in sync. Almost simultaneous.

Antoine turned to him. "Well? Do your thing, Web! I got this."

Nikifor moved to Steven and Nyura. "We need an exit strategy. Think you two can handle that?"

Nyura nodded. "There's a pair of armored vehicles we can use, but we'll need a hole."

Nikifor replied, "Leave that to us. We can regroup at the Arsenal."

Steven glared. "I thought we agreed that was in the bad ideas category?"

Sighing, Nikifor snapped. "We don't have the advantage you think we have. No fence, lots of gunfire to attract hostiles, and three people not fit to run. And yes, you're included in that."

Steven said, "Right now, we have the benefit of being in an entrenched position. They have to come to us. We should get Antoine and Brice on the roof, and hold here. Two snipers gives plenty of coverage for us to fight back."

"How much extra ammunition did you bring? We've got at least two squads, and who knows how many Talons are on the way?"

Steven waved absently at the other room. "There's plenty here. But if we're quick about punching through, we shouldn't have to worry about it."

Nikifor pointed up toward the roof. "If the enemy has sniper teams deployed, we're outflanked."

Growling, Steven's eyes flashed dark thoughts. "Unless they're rocking anti-materiel rifles like Antoine, you guys should be fine. We can keep you covered from ground level."

"Then only one sniper can be on the roof. And we still end up outmaneuvered. I like how you're thinking," said Nikifor, sighing. "I really do. But you need to assume the enemy is competent. They came to us, and they're not going to wait for us to figure it all out. Right now, the priority needs to be getting the civilians and wounded out of harm's way."

Steven hissed. "That's the whole damn point I'm making. Lure the enemy into this kill box, instead of driving us into another one."

"Get the hell down that ladder!" Steven yelled, taking a position behind the vehicle.

Nikifor aimed his rifle at the new hole as he moved to get between the enemies and the group. A grenade arced into the room. Brice fired his rifle at the grenade. The bullet punched through the grenade's body, breaking it apart into useless metal and spilled explosive compound.

Black-clothed figures rushed in, firing as they moved. Three went around the other side of one of the armored vehicles. Two others curved toward him. Nikifor and Steven fired back. The two commandos went down after several shots from each. A figure appeared behind Steven, leveling a rifle at his head. Nikifor's heart leapt into his throat. *No way he can react in time, and I don't have a clear shot.*

"Steven, look out!" Curtis speared into the enemy, tackling him to the ground. He struggled with the enemy for only a moment before he was overpowered. Steven turned just in time to watch the enemy soldier ram a knife into Curtis's gut, and the young man gasped, falling to the side before the soldier pulled a pistol and shot him in the chest.

Steven fired a bullet into the enemy soldier's forehead. He moved to the other side of the vehicle swiftly, firing two more shots. The garage settled into an uneasy quiet for just a few moments, aside from the howling of Talons getting closer, and commando's boots scraping the pavement outside.

Steven stared at Curtis's body as he moved toward the sewer entrance, a stricken expression on his face. Four more bodies lay by the open cover, blood pooling around them. They had been part of the group Nikifor had brought in from the street. *We took too long. What the hell did I save them for, if this is where they'll all die? They need time they don't have.*

"Screw this," said Nikifor, growling. "Get them out."

Nikifor grimaced, channeling his brother's fury as he rushed out into the night with a warrior's scream. Four helmets snapped his direction and the enemies fired. A bullet glanced off his shoulder plate. He turned and fired his rifle several times. The enemies moved to cover almost as one being. *I only hit one. They're good.* The commando's arm hung, bleeding from the shoulder. The soldier switched to a pistol with such swiftness, Nikifor might as well have shot him with a wad of moist paper.

Nikifor scoffed, "What the hell?"

Something punched into his armor. Pain radiated throughout his body with every new breath, blurring his vision and causing him to curse in surprise.

He rolled to the opposite building, hugging the wall as he continued firing at the approaching soldiers. Two of the three fell before his rifle ran dry. He let the rifle dangle from its strap and searched the skyline. A spinning green triangle drew his attention to a rooftop just a block away. *That would be the sniper.*

Nikifor drew his suppressed Kimber and rushed the final soldier in his way. The shots the soldier got off glanced off the armor, and Nikifor threw a heavy punch to his jaw. The man's head shook and he stepped back.

Following up, Nikifor kicked the soldier's leg, dropping him to a knee. He shoved his Kimber into the soldier's chin and squeezed the trigger, staring in the direction of the sniper as the soldier in his hands fell limp.

Nikifor moved, low and swift, as another shot impacted nearby. He moved in a serpentine fashion until he reached the burning wreckage of the enemy vehicle. The sniper fired off a shot every fifteen seconds or so. *He doesn't care that he's missing. He's dialing me in, though, for sure. Shot spacing seems semi-automatic. Maybe a Dragunov?*

A Talon dropped from the rooftop to his left; Nikifor dodged around the twisted metal, popping two shots into the creature's nose. His chest burned deep with the motion. He smiled wryly.

At least it doesn't feel broken. I know that pain intimately. Thanks, Joseph.

The rib was severely bruised, then. Possibly cracked. Nikifor spared a moment to glance at the spot that had been hit. His armor cracked right where the rib would be, the deformed rifle round embedded in the plate.

He hustled through the storage lot and across to the building the shots had come from, every breath and movement stretched sharp pain across his chest. Talons howled behind and ahead. Their screams filled the air around him. He smiled as he slipped a small, flat disc from the pouch on his thigh. He slapped it on the wall corner. Pressing a button on his databrace, he turned and bounded down the alleyway.

Nikifor hopped on top of a dumpster, turned, and pushed, clearing the edge of the fire escape. A pair of Talons turned the corner, and the device on the wall exploded in steel shards, cutting them down. He surged up the stairs of the fire escape.

A shot zipped past his head as he emerged onto the roof and rolled. The sniper had no spotter. Sloppy, but still dangerous enough. Perhaps the enemy didn't have the numbers for full deployment. Or the spotter was waiting for him to commit to the engagement.

He aimed at a point on the sniper's upper arm and shot once. The man's arm dropped his rifle clattering to the ground.

He pulled a pistol with his other hand, but Nikifor shot through the wrist, and he dropped that as well.

The sniper rushed forward and swung a wild haymaker. The move was awkwardly executed with the busted wrist and the other arm flopping like a fish. Nikifor sidestepped and tripped him, kneeling on the writhing man's chest.

Nikifor swept the rooftop with his Kimber, counting a full minute as the sniper beneath his knee struggled against him and his armor.

Nikifor reached down and unsnapped the man's featureless black helmet. Removing it, he revealed a face that was hauntingly empty of emotion. All the thrashing was right, but there was no feeling behind it.

"Who, or what the hell are you?" Nikifor asked.

Instead of answering, the sniper went still. He flexed his jaw, which issued a crunch. He convulsed for a few minutes and lay still again. Dead.

Nikifor cursed, looking down into the alley where Talons had begun to gather. One of them sniffed at the bodies of the fallen, tilting its head back and forth as though confused.

He moved to the sniper's dropped rifle. The rifle's synthetic black body shone in the light from streetlights below. Ejecting the magazine, he inspected the ammunition. The cartridge had a sharp, hardened steel core. He winced. It was no wonder it had done so much damage. Armor-piercing seven point six-two millimeter round from what was essentially a fancy Kalashnikov sniper rifle. Korean characters marked the stamped metal receiver. A small crate sat open nearby, brimming with unused magazines.

Nikifor activated his radio. "Cross, you still there?"

"Yeah," Joseph replied. "Did you guys get away alright?"

Grimacing, Nikifor said, "Five civilian casualties. I led the rest of the danger away while the others got out. They shouldn't be too long."

"You gonna make it to the party?"

"Not without a big can of bug spray. These guys we were taking fire from are carrying North Korean military gear. And the sniper I took down is nowhere close to looking Asian. I'll hold out here for a bit; get to me when you can."

Maurice spoke up, "Understood. Stay safe, Web."

Nikifor leaned over the roof ledge, aiming the rifle carefully. He squeezed the trigger, the rattling blast accompanied by the spray of blood from a Talon's head. He switched targets and fired again before the first finished falling.

<u>14 Choices</u>

The stench of the sewer burned Steven's eyes and throat. He stalked at the front of the group in ankle-deep, muddy-looking water, his Glock at the ready. Valko walked beside him, cradling Pattie in one arm like a toddler, her arms draped around his neck. Antoine sauntered on Valko's other side.

"How do you do it?" asked Valko. Steven was shocked at how softly Valko had spoken.

Steven shook his head, trying to process the question. "Walk through the sewer without a filtration system? Mostly spite."

Valko chuckled, somewhat muffled through the helmet. "Not what I meant, smartass."

Steven laughed too, grimacing at the pain in his abdomen. "So, I'm a smartass dumbass? Good to know."

"Steven!" Valko hissed, voice ragged and strained. "Look, this is a serious question. I know you and Curtis had your differences. After everything that's happened, how are you still going like this?"

Steven shrugged, glancing back at Grace. "It's simple, really. I picked a reason to fight. I'll have plenty of time to debate that or regret his sacrifice later. After she's safe."

"Why would he do that, anyway? Didn't he hate you?"

Steven slowed his pace, contemplating. "I don't think he ever actually hated me. I scared him. People either attack or run from the things they're afraid of. That's just nature itself."

He looked back again. Grace walked arm in arm with her father, eyes downcast as she spoke to him quietly. She smiled softly and blushed when she noticed Steven looking her way.

Her father, for his part, scowled and gripped his shotgun tighter.

"Honestly," said Steven, turning back to Valko, "I think I get what you're actually asking. You never forget the bad things. You just learn to live in the numb moments. Find comfort where you can."

Valko half shrugged. "That doesn't explain much."

"Point is," said Steven, rubbing his face, "it's all choices. Life, death, love. None of it is random. All of it is a choice."

Antoine laughed from Valko's other side. "So, you're not dead because you're choosing not to die? What kind of answer is that?"

Steven glared back at Antoine. "The more people there are involved with the choice, of course, the more complicated the solution becomes. I'm choosing to fight to keep them safe. But that choice could lead to death. I had the option to run and save my own life. To choose is to have power."

"Yeah," Antoine intoned. "Screw all that philosophical mumbo jumbo. My power is stuffed into a brass casing behind a heavy-ass fifty-caliber lead spike. Whatever, or whoever, is on the other side when I pull the trigger? Yeah, they don't get to choose nothing else."

"I'm not sure you have the capacity to understand how wrong you are."

Scoffing, Antoine said, "No? Listen up, puke. You're a weapon. A killer. What were the choices that brought us here? The only one I can think of is 'don't die'."

"Maybe we didn't have the choices then. But we can make them now."

"Are you even listening to me?" Antoine snapped. "Are you listening to yourself? You whine and mope about how bad your life is, how bad of a person you are, and now you're saying it's all a choice? Pick a lane, and own that shit! No wonder people don't like you. Pathetic son of a bitch."

Steven's eyes narrowed sharply, and he turned to face Antoine. The group halted behind them at the face-off. Valko stepped back to get Pattie from between them. In Steven's peripheral, Grace clutched her father's hand, breath held. Steven pulled in a breath as deeply as possible. The pain was unbearable. His fingers flexed on the Glock's grip, tighter with every heartbeat. Grace's words came back to him. *Why waste energy on his pettiness, when it's the same energy you need to use to fight?*

Antoine chimed, laughing. "What's wrong, puke? You going to cry now? You going to pretend you have a right to be angry when I'm just repeating the same crap I've heard you say to yourself?"

Smiling, Steven released his pent-up breath and loosened his grip on the gun. "I'm going to pretend you aren't just hiding your own fear behind all these snide comments. Tell you what, though. If we make it out of this, I don't mind proving myself and kicking your ass then."

Antoine tilted his head. "Huh. I hope that little bit of spine you're showing now doesn't fail you when the real shit hits us."

"The real shit?" Valko scoffed. "That fresh scratch on your helmet should have reminded you to be humble. You're hiding behind painted steel, while the rest of them are literally standing in the *real* shit."

Steven turned away, unsatisfied, but trying not to let himself get too riled up again. He reaffirmed a calm rhythm through measured breaths. His body ached in so many places. Deep, pulsing aches that made his arms and legs feel like lead weights. Every movement was a battle, every breath a victory. He needed to save what strength he had left for the real fight.

Looking back, Grace gave him a thumbs up and a raised eyebrow. He relaxed his grip. "While we're just walking through the sewer, Valko, I think I'll take a short rest."

"Sounds good. There's more pushing to do before this clears, and I need you ready for that. Country Mile, you've got point."

Antoine sighed but ranged ahead without a retort. *A possible indication of growth? Maybe boredom?*

Steven sagged as he glanced around the group. His breath was still quick and shallow unless he made a conscious effort to breathe normally. It took so much concentration just to breathe.

Valko put his free hand on Steven's shoulder. "Hey, you good?"

Steven nodded slowly.

Valko held his gaze for a bit. "Seriously. Let me know if you need to actually rest. We can always give point to Brice or Nyura. Country Mile can carry Pattie, and I can carry you."

Steven chuckled, glancing at Grace again. "No offense, but no thank you. I'd rather have Pattie with someone I can trust. I could use some backup with Grace, though."

"Oh?" said Valko, a hint of a chuckle in his voice. "I think you've got that covered."

Forcing a grin, Steven said, "You say that, but let's be real. There aren't many worse ways to meet a girl's parents than in the middle of a sewer with a gun in your hand."

Valko laughed and clapped him on the shoulder. Hard. Steven winced, grunting under the blow.

Valko held his hand up. "Ah, my bad."

Steven gritted his teeth, giving a thumbs up. "It's all good. I'm just glad you have a real sense of humor."

Valko nodded and turned to follow Antoine in leading the group. They all began trudging through the muck again. Steven waited a moment, slipping his Glock into a pocket and extending his hand to Grace's father.

"Hi," he said, hesitating. "I'm Steven."

Grace raised an eyebrow in question.

What the hell? I can face a street full of ravenous monsters without flinching, but I'm scared enough of Grace's dad that I'm making things super awkward?

"Robert," the man grumbled before accepting the hand. He tilted his head to the side, indicating the nearby woman walking with Mirena. "My wife, Rachel."

Steven nodded to her and turned back to Robert. "I really wish we were all meeting under better circumstances."

"Is now really the time for this?"

I must look like a real bonehead right now. Might as well tell the truth, right?

Steven frowned, the pain in his sides a steep reminder of how close he'd come to being disemboweled. "Considering my day so far, this is the only time I'll get."

Grace reached out, eyes wide. She embraced Steven. His head swam, and he grunted from the pressure. Robert's eyes narrowed, and he clenched his jaw.

"What did I say, Steven?" she whispered. "Be nicer to yourself, please."

Smiling, Steven returned the hug under Robert's watchful glare. "This isn't about that. I just know my odds." He sighed at her glare. "Who knows? Maybe I'll be pleasantly wrong. Maybe

I'll see the end of this thing. We can really figure out what's between us at that point."

Grace's eyes seemed impossibly wider as her face reddened.

Robert cleared his throat. His face had softened. He pushed at his short, dirty-blonde hair with a beefy hand. He was tall, relatively muscular, but not in shape. He adjusted the shattered glasses on his face.

"I'm inclined to believe my daughter is right about you," he said. "But let's be clear. I don't trust you."

Steven shrugged. "That's fair."

Robert said, "No, it's really not. But I'm willing to be unfair to you if it keeps my daughter safe. All I know about you is what she's said. Speaking of, since you're insisting, I think the two of us need to have a real discussion."

Grace looked up sharply, narrowing her eyes at her father. Robert shook his head and waved her on. As the others passed by, Steven leaned against the wall of smoothed concrete.

"You're really hurting, aren't you?" Robert asked.

Steven nodded. "If it wasn't for Nyura, my day would have ended before sunset."

"Was it that bad?"

"That school went to hell in minutes," said Steven softly. "Every teacher that didn't change into a monster was ripped to shreds by one that did. A lot of people died there, and we were lucky to make it out. Even with the gun."

Steven absently touched the cut on his cheek. *Probably better not to mention Dr. Harper.*

Robert rubbed a hand across his chin. "That's the other part that has me concerned."

Steven spoke slowly. "Until lives were at stake, the gun stayed hidden. The threat we're under should make my possession of it irrelevant."

Robert pointed a finger. "It really doesn't, though. It was irresponsible and illegal. Someone your age shouldn't have had access to begin with. Intentions are well and good, but the road to hell is paved with good intentions, buddy."

"Yeah, Hogan and Abaroa quoted that to me daily as well." Steven said, rubbing his face. "Look, I've been having a really bad time today, especially given the whole gun thing. So, I'm not trying anymore."

Robert Peterson stared at Steven for a long moment, eyes half-narrowed. It was unlikely anyone had taken that kind of tone with him in a long time. Steven had seen more intimidating scowls before, though, and it appeared half-hearted.

Robert tilted his chin, indicating ahead of them. "If I'm being honest, it's more telling that you restrained yourself with the rifle guy."

Steven looked at the older man, with his graying, stubbly, square chin. "You can blame Grace for that. She hasn't led me wrong yet. I know that she's more special than I can understand. I don't deserve her attention, and I never could."

Grace's eyes went wide, then softened as she broke into a small smile and averted her gaze. Steven hadn't spotted her coming back. Nyura and Brice were with her.

Robert's lips pinched together, and he blew a heavy breath. "Well, now," he said, with a sly half-smile. "You're not leaving me a lot of room to dislike you."

Steven shook his head. "That's not what this is about. I just-"

"You want me to understand what she means to you," Robert said.

Steven nodded.

"We'll need to talk more, but for now you've got my thanks, and my trust." Robert held out the shotgun to him. "You'll probably know how to use this thing better than I can. It's gotta be better than your pistol, right?"

Steven shook his head, "No, I'm not much of a shot with those. Besides, the force from it would rip my stitches." He chuckled. "Nyura would kick my ass."

Brice piped up, "Yeah. You should see him with that pistol, though. Absolutely phenomenal."

Steven rolled his eyes and groaned. "Not helping, Brice."

"He just wants to remind you he's here," Nyura giggled. "Poor guy's got a rifle and still can't catch up."

"Hey!" Brice said. "You shut your dirty mouth."

Nyura punched him in the shoulder. "Don't pretend you could make me."

Brice shook his head. "Somebody needs to wake Pattie up, so Nyura can stop picking on me."

Grace snorted and covered her mouth to stifle the laugh.

Robert returned his shotgun to its previous position, one eyebrow raised at the antics around him. They walked on in silence for a while. The end of the tunnel came into sight. Antoine and Valko stood at the base of the ladder to the surface, ready.

Steven retrieved his Glock from his pocket. "Alright. Back to work for us. I don't know where we're coming up, so be ready for anything."

Valko waited until they got closer, then looked at Robert. "Hey, could I get you to carry Pattie for a moment?"

Robert nodded, passing the shotgun to his wife. She held the gun in trembling fingers until Nyura relieved her of it and put it into a safer position. Valko passed Pattie to Robert, who cradled her in his arms. She looked so small, curled up like she was.

Steven said, "What are we walking into?"

Valko shrugged. "No clue. Considering what happened at the safe house, we should be ready for just about anything. I'll go up first, Antoine follows. The rest of you should be safe enough to follow up afterward."

15 Destiny

Joseph stared around the communications room at the various towers of blinking server computers. Trying desperately not to consider the consequences of fighting the Akuma. The Akuma's claw had ripped through Maurice's armor like it'd been made of toilet paper.

Maurice sat there, typing furiously, breathing in ragged gasps as he restored downed communications systems and recovered data from wiped hard drives. Around his abdomen was a bandage, almost soaked through. Something caught Joseph's eyes. A familiar face. Burnished copper hair. Hazel eyes.

Mom.

"Wisp," Joseph whispered. "Go back. What was that?"

Maurice clicked back a screen. It was a military dossier on his mother. Joseph hadn't seen that face in years, except in his dreams. The dossier contained her vital information, as well as some of the combat feats she'd achieved while an Army Ranger. The notation at the bottom of the screen froze his blood.

Suitable template. Psychological profile suggests the subject is prone to Post-Traumatic Stress. The subject also, however, shows strong willpower in ignoring the symptoms without medical and therapeutic aids. Currently single. Two children aged seven and four, respectively. Update: Template deceased, children acquired for Nomad Initiative (See attached documentation for operations report).

Joseph didn't remember holding his breath, but his chest started burning with the exertion. He exhaled and brought in another breath, but only rage entered his body.

"Were you able to get the operations reports?"

Maurice nodded. Some of the color had returned to his face. He set the entire group of recovered files to copy, then switched to the page Joseph wanted.

Joseph was grateful for the helmet covering his features. He'd never cried in front of his men before. He wasn't going to let them see it now. He pulled in a deep breath as he read.

"They planned it all," he whispered. "They killed her. Forced me to make my first kill. They broke us all, and for what?"

Maurice clicked a link on the report. A voice sounded through the speakers on the computer. "It's time to collect the Nomad and Special Operations candidates."

"Shouldn't we be using the adults?" Blackwood's voice came through the speaker.

Someone else's voice said, "So sentimental. Just like every other old soldier. I need weapons to test. But to build them, I need to break them first. Breaking adults is far too time-consuming. I need these children. Specifically, these. You need to get them. I've listed the templates for you. All you need to do is arrange for their collection."

"You call me sentimental?" Blackwood. "You're the one with your wife in a glass jar."

"Oh? Would you like me to let her out? I'm sure she'd love to meet you, Blackwood," the first voice said, sounding gleeful as a child.

Blackwood coughed nervously. "Point taken. I'll get them, and I'll keep my thoughts on your methods to myself."

"That would be best."

"What about Chavez's order?"

"He'll get his doses. The new formula should make him happy. A tad more autonomy, but the same level of control.

Now his pet hounds can stop shitting themselves just because he didn't order them not to."

The recording apparently ended, leaving Joseph listening to the rhythm of his own breathing. He shook his head and turned back to Maurice. "What the hell was that?"

Maurice said, "Portion of a recovered audio file. It's likely the only one I'll be able to restore."

"Save everything you can to an external source or three," said Joseph. "These bastards are going to roast for what they did to us."

16 Cost of Secrets

Steven and the others emerged beneath a hazy night sky, feet from the Arsenal gates. A pile of Talon-type corpses lay in the center of the Arsenal parking lot. The Nomads had been thorough. Across the campus, in front of another building, more bodies were strewn about like broken dolls.

Joseph walked out of the building, supporting Maurice with a shoulder. They trudged across the lot, their bodies tense. A concerning shade of red covered Maurice's lower torso. Just around the soaked cloth, the armor looked as if it had been cut. Small cracks ringed what had to have been impact points where the cuts started.

"Nyura," said Steven. "Can you help him?"

Nyura nodded. "I can try. That's a lot of blood."

Valko and Nikifor hurried over and supported Maurice the remaining distance. Joseph took his helmet off and stalked to the group. Steven couldn't remember seeing this much hurt and anger in anyone's eyes. And yet, the red-rimmed eyes and pursed lips betrayed him. He'd been crying.

"We have a problem," Joseph said, looking at each of the Nomads and Operators. "Everything we thought we'd been saved from to be brought here. It was all orchestrated by Richards and Blackwood."

Steven narrowed his eyes. "What, exactly, does that mean?"

"The scar on your chest," Joseph snapped. "It was all planned. The traumas we went through as kids. The fire you guys were under; it's the same group that killed your parents and scarred you for life. They. Work. For. Richards."

Steven's chest tightened with a suddenly hammering pulse. He found himself trembling.

Valko sucked his teeth. "That would explain Blackwood not wanting to call in backup. Do you think they had those commandos on call to sanitize the project?"

Joseph dropped his helmet on the pile of corpses. "My thoughts exactly," he said, staring down at the bodies. "Their experiment failed. Now, they need the evidence to go away."

Harper's words came to mind. *I didn't let Richards program my dose of the virus, so I'm not driven to kill. Unless I want to be.* Steven crossed his arms. "No. That's only partially right."

Joseph chuckled. "Oh, yeah? What are you thinking?"

"Harper did something to shake things up. I'm not sure what, but he accelerated their timeline to the breaking point. Everything's been thrown out of balance, and we just happen to be caught in the middle of it."

Joseph gestured wildly, pulling a thumb drive from a pouch. "There's no such thing as 'wrong place, wrong time' when a kill-squad or two tears down your fence and hurls rounds at you. They're called the Alcydes's Hounds--a containment procedure. They've got a pre-programmed version of the nano-virus. They're completely controlled. We were the weapons with free will. A test to see if we'd make better soldiers. With things breaking down, anyone with a trace of the nano-virus is their target. And take a wild guess at why you're still standing right now."

Steven shrugged. "Probably because I'm stubborn as hell."

Joseph scowled. "No, puke. You carry a successful iteration of the virus. I hate that this is true, but you're just a fancy version of the Talon-types, buddy. You have a faster than normal healing rate, and a heightened fight or flight response. And the Nomads are that, plus experimental armor and weaponry. You and Pattie are alive because of the nano-virus in your blood."

Steven jabbed a finger at the girl in Robert's arms. "So, why is she still unconscious? Or, more importantly, why am I not?"

"Probably--like you said--because you're stubborn as hell." Throwing his hands up in bewildered frustration, Joseph grunted. He sat on the pile of corpses, next to his helmet. He held his head in his hands, breathing deep.

He spoke softly. "Look, Steven. I'm sorry, but we've been played. Each of us was tested. Traumatic stress response and combat effectiveness. These are the secrets you fought your way here to get. I hope they're worth the losses for you. Because it's starting to look like shit to me."

Steven chuckled sadly. *Curtis would have loved laughing in my face about this one.* Turning back to Joseph, he said, "So let's fix their mistake and put an end to the program."

Joseph smiled sadly. "Who gave you permission to be the voice of reason on this base?"

Steven grinned. "There's nothing reasonable about what I'm saying." He glanced sidelong at Grace's worried face. "But since someone's gone through the trouble to convince me I'm not a monster, I'd like to see what life is like without all this crap attached."

Joseph lifted his helmet with care, grinning. "You know, you've got a point. Then, as my first act as true commander of this unit, I'd like to offer congratulations on your promotion, Nomad. Specialist Steven Joseph Fuller, operational call sign: Sage."

Steven swayed, eyes wide as the earth seemed to tilt out of view.

Joseph chuckled. "Don't look so surprised, Sage. If I'd been in command in the first place, you'd have earned your place among us years ago."

Antoine scoffed. "And me? You told me a few days ago you'd replace me with him if you could."

Eyes narrowed; Joseph mulled over his own words. "You were harassing my sister. If I had my way, I'd have killed you for what you did to her. As it stands, we can't afford to fight amongst ourselves. We have to survive the night first. After that, I'm more than willing to simply part ways with you."

Steven crossed his arms. "Time for the next step, then. Capture and detain Blackwood and Richards. Find a way to put an end to this."

Joseph held up a finger. "I've got some good news on that front. Blackwood and Abaroa should be joining us out here any minute. I let them know a few minutes ago. A National Guard detachment and a joint government task force are on their way into the city. They'll clear the rest of the city for us, and gather Nikifor on their way. We just need to do our part with the other two."

Two shapes emerged from the command building. Abaroa led. Blackwood followed with hands held behind his back. *He looks too secure. He's expecting a confrontation. What the hell do you have planned, Blackwood?*

Maurice pushed away from Nyura, pulling his pistol and pointing it at Blackwood. Blackwood smiled mischievously, reaching out and wrapping an arm around Abaroa's throat. Abaroa attempted to resist, but Blackwood kicked the back of the younger man's knee and pulled him in close. The other hand was still behind his back.

Too soon. Maurice, dammit. You moved too soon.

Seven weapons were aimed at Blackwood. Each of the Nomad and Special Operations members with steady hands and eyes. Blackwood still smiled. Abaroa narrowed his eyes and locked eyes with Steven. He nodded, as though an understanding passed between them.

"Stand down, children," Blackwood said. There was no menace. No pleading. Only his usual commanding presence. When they made no move to comply, he continued, "I am ordering you to lower your weapons and stand down."

Maurice scoffed. "Let go of Abaroa and allow us to take you into custody, sir. Don't pretend we won't shoot through him if you don't. You trained us better than that. Now, let him go and put your hands up."

Blackwood glared at Maurice and swung his hidden hand around. He pulled the trigger of the large caliber pistol in his grip. Maurice sent a shot that glanced across the top of Blackwood's shoulder.

Steven fought not to turn at the sounds of screaming behind him. Grace's voice was among the cacophony. A large dent appeared in the back of Maurice's helmet, and he dropped with a crash to the pavement. Blood oozed from the shattered remnants of the helmet's glass visor.

Blackwood seethed through clenched teeth, "I will execute every single one of you if you don't get in line and start following orders. Stand. Down!"

Steven's heart pounded in his ears as Blackwood swung the heavy pistol around, aiming at one person, then another. He was well hidden behind Abaroa. Not an easy shot to take without harming Abaroa. No one blamed Abaroa for their plight, and they'd rather not kill him, but it was only a matter of time before someone started shooting. Only one choice. A split second to decide.

"Take cover," yelled Steven, rushing to the side, away from the group of civilians behind him.

Abaroa's eyes went wide as Steven advanced. Steven stepped to a blind spot as Blackwood took a shot. He hadn't planned on having his vision limited by his hostage. Blackwood grunted and shoved Abaroa.

Steven leaped over Abaroa and came down with a kick to Blackwood's gun hand. The gun clattered to the ground and Blackwood pulled a knife with his now free hand. The pain in Steven's gut made him wince and hesitate.

Blackwood swung the blade at an alarming speed. Steven whirled with the motion, catching his wrist and twisting. Blackwood slammed his forehead down into Steven's face.

Steven's nose exploded in pain, and his vision became starry and bright. Eyes watering, Steven punched the Glock forward into Blackwood's gut. Blackwood parried the gun to the side as Steven squeezed the trigger.

Hopping back from the missed shot, Steven pulled his arms into the close quarters position, as Blackwood eyed his surroundings in a controlled sweep. He feinted with the knife, making Steven dodge to the side, where he threw a hook.

Steven put his arm up just in time to block the blow, though it sent a painful shock through his system. The knife came a moment later, biting into Steven's side. The path it carved left a sharp pain that seemed to sear through Steven's core.

The others were moving into position, but they were still too far away to get a clean shot, and if he moved too far away, Blackwood would have an opportunity to go for his gun.

Gritting his teeth, that familiar cloyingly metallic and tart taste coating his tongue, Steven slipped into the numb enjoyment of combat. He shoved his heavy boot into Blackwood's thigh. The older man grunted, but pushed forward, grabbing hold of Steven's waist. He seized Steven's gun arm with his other hand and headbutted again.

Vision clouded, Steven tilted the gun, firing blindly into Blackwood. The older man let go and staggered back, face contorted. Steven punched the gun out, into the man's chest and squeezed the trigger again and again. Each shot made Blackwood stagger back another inch or two, but as his shirt shredded, the body armor showed through clearer.

After four or so more shots, Steven aimed from a combat position and planted three quick, clean shots into Blackwood's forehead. Blackwood dropped, falling to the side with a soft sound. His body twitched several times, then fell still.

Chest heaving, Steven wiped blood from his mouth onto his shirt and stumbled back. Everything hurt like hell. In the silence, there was so much to hear. The way people exhaled into the cooling night air told him some of them had been anxious, afraid. He let the stress bleed from his lungs, pulling in another breath.

His eyes swept the lot, Glock held ready. He glanced back at Abaroa, who held the side of his head with a trembling hand. Blood trickled from under the hand, likely coming from his ear.

Grace's mother, Rachel, and Nyura moved to Abaroa, pulling him back to a clear spot where they checked him over for more immediately treatable wounds.

"Don't worry about me," said Abaroa, staring slack-jawed at Steven. "Thank you."

"I'm here for answers," Steven squinted at Abaroa.

"As far as the paperwork, he's as clueless as we were." Joseph said, earning a glance from Abaroa.

"What's that supposed to mean?" asked Abaroa, "What's this all about?"

Relaxing his grip on the Glock, Steven said, "We'll fill you in later, sir. Think Richards will come easier?"

Contemplating, Joseph said, "Considering the circumstances, maybe not. But he shouldn't have anyone to take hostage, either. One thing before that, though."

Valko shifted. "Shouldn't we wait for Web?"

Joseph whispered. "He'd be here if he could. We need to keep moving."

Nodding, Valko knelt with Joseph by Maurice's body. Antoine stepped over and stood behind them. The two placed a hand each on him, and Antoine turned his rifle to the ground, resting his hands on its butt.

"As we face the sunset," said Joseph.

"We give service in honor," Valko responded.

"As we face the sunrise," said Joseph.

"We have hope in brotherhood," Antoine recited.

"And when we face our judgment," Joseph challenged, a dangerous edge to his voice.

"We find victory in sacrifice," Valko said, an air of finality to the words.

A hollow silence settled on the night. Steven hung his head for a moment reverently, committing the words to memory.

Valko growled. "Let's go get Richards. You guys have access to the labs?"

"No, but Blackwood certainly did." Joseph took the pock-marked ID card from a lanyard on Blackwood's pocket, holding it up. He smiled appreciatively at Steven through the single bullet hole on the side of the card. "Sage, coordinate these people. I hear you're good at that."

Steven pointed. "Kathryn, get these civilians into the dormitory building. Antoine and Brice are on overwatch. Nyura, take Abaroa to the dorm infirmary. Joseph and Valko with me to the lab. Let's give the National Guard less to clean up."

17 Hollow

Some days waking up is hell enough. Molly trudged doggedly down the highway. All she knew was the pain of waking up nearby a crushed SUV, surrounded by bodies. Her mouth was dry and chalky, her steps unsure. She had picked up the rifle by reflex, then limped off into the woods on her own. The damn thing was heavy and growing heavier with every step. *Why am I even carrying it? I don't want this thing.*

She'd been walking so long, time had lost meaning to her. Had it been hours? Days? Her feet were covered in sharp aches, as though something were being shoved through the skin. But she never stopped. She couldn't bring herself to stop. And the more she tried, the more things within broke, leaving behind a hollow determination with no real reasoning behind it.

"Where am I going?" asked Molly, her limbs leaden and thoughts in a fog as she walked on. The distinct glow of a fire lit the horizon ahead of her. Her heart began thumping with more intensity. The hollow inside shifted, becoming danger; perhaps purpose. A dark green Honda sedan caught her eye. "That car. That's my target. Why?"

Molly raised her rifle instinctively as she approached the Honda. This was the place she'd been led. There was something within the car, calling her forward. Her body grew excited, muscles flexing in rapid succession, preparing for action. Adrenaline surged, eliminating all pain, leaving only the desire to kill.

The car door burst open, and a girl emerged. Her hair was red and tangled. She looked wild and afraid. The girl's glittering green eyes narrowed as she approached the combat with haste. She held something small and metallic in her hand. Molly recognized her as an immediate threat. Not only a threat, but a target. Molly leveled the rifle at the girl's chest and squeezed the trigger.

The red-haired girl hopped to the side as she ran, avoiding the shot. Molly took several more shots, the rifle bucking into her tired shoulder. Shots went wild, hitting all but Molly's intended target. Her reasons were still unclear. Fear filtered through her body, returning strength and speed as it coursed. Molly stopped trying to aim, positioning her barrel ahead of where the girl ran, squeezing the trigger again. The rifle was out of bullets.

The red-haired girl executed an expert roundhouse kick, knocking the rifle from Molly's hands. The metal object in her hand flashed, and pain shot across Molly's arm as she blocked the blow. The red-haired girl pulled back the screwdriver, dripping with crimson. She bared her teeth, lashing out again with a scream. Molly parried the blow and planted a fist in the girl's gut, ending her scream in a gasp.

The two girls traded blows, neither backing down. Molly's blood spattered from lacerations and a split lip. She tackled the red-haired girl, wrenching the screwdriver from her hand. She plunged it at the other girl's eye, her hand stopping short. The girl had blocked the attack. The girl's eyes were wide, and she grunted in exertion.

"Who are you?" Molly cried. Her tears dripped from her chin, mingled with blood, onto the other girl's face. "Why do I want to kill you? Why do I want it so bad? Why can't I stop fighting you?"

A strange look crossed the red-haired girl's face. Molly couldn't process the expression. The girl's eyes had softened with tears, and her lips quivered. She narrowed her moist eyes and snapped several rapid punches into Molly's gut. Blood from Molly's mouth spattered on the dark pavement beside the girl's head. The girl shoved, knocking Molly off her. She straddled Molly and stabbed into her chest with the screwdriver.

Pain exploded in Molly's chest, bringing with it a certain clarity. The red-haired girl ran an arm over her face, wiping away tears and blood. She was beautiful, with her piercing emerald eyes and freckled face. And then, Molly recognized the expression on her opponent's face: sorrow. It reminded Molly of her sister. The day was far too clear. The blood coating her knife. Her sister's sad eyes with their fading light. Another explosion of pain rocked Molly as the screwdriver plunged down again.

"I'll likely never know your name," said the red-haired girl, sniffing back a sob. "But I'm sorry. I can't let you stop me."

Molly's vision went black moments after seeing the bloody tip of the screwdriver approaching. The pain was incredible, but only for a moment. She shuddered as the darkness accepted her. Truly accepted her. The silence brought peace with it. A peace she'd never known.

18 How Things End

Emily straddled the body of the brown-haired girl, hands fallen to her sides. She pulled in heavy breaths, fighting against the sobs that tried to shake her. Something had been wrong with this girl. She had somehow survived the crash in Tennessee, only to walk for days to this point just outside Blue Rock.

A deep, thrumming sound filled the air. Emily needed to move. That sound could only be a helicopter.

The girl had looked wild, with her matted brown hair. Broken bones in her mousy face. Her clothing had been shredded and her limbs were covered in blood. Something had changed, however, when she'd gotten close to where Emily had hunkered down for a quick rest. The girl had burst into action, as though her exhaustion and shattered body were immaterial.

Emily turned away from the girl's broken face. It wouldn't do to keep staring at the screwdriver handle protruding from between the poor girl's eyes. Where had Emily seen that half-crazed, hollow look before? There was something far too familiar about it. Far too familiar about the way the girl fought.

No emotion. Machine-like. A pain stabbed at Emily's chest. Steven fought like that. The more he got hurt, the more his eyes took on that dead look. *What was this?* Emily wondered for a moment at what the connection could be.

She needed to get into the city and find her brother first. She could ask questions and hash things out after she was sure of his survival.

Abruptly, light bathed the area around her, and she covered her eyes against the glare. Car doors swung open, and people emerged. She saw the unmistakable movements that meant guns tracked her position. There were too many of them. She had neither the strength nor the cover left to make it against that many. *How to get away?*

"Emily?" Sean's voice. "I made it clear what needed to happen, kid. This isn't the way to save your brother."

Emily's eyes burned as she stood, ripping the screwdriver from the girl's forehead. The wet sound made bile rise in Emily's throat. The metal dripped blood as she got into a fighting stance. She couldn't regulate her breathing enough. She needed to bury the sobs. Bury the emotion. Find that dead zone Steven and the now slain girl seemed to have mastered.

Emily imagined shoving the emotions behind a door. It didn't work, so she gave a crooked, toothy smile from the painful place she'd found herself. "You must've missed me. I see you brought backup, but no burger. I'm honestly starving. You should have brought the burger."

"Stop this, Emily." Candace's voice came from one of the silhouettes. "We're not here to hurt you. We want all of you safe. But we can't make that happen unless you let us help."

Lies. These agents were full of lies. They couldn't help her. How could they, when it would likely require them to fight against weaponized children? This was perhaps the thing that made Emily hesitate to gather the guns and fight back at the diner. A mistake she'd corrected now.

"And how, exactly, can you help?" Emily growled into the blinding lights ahead of her.

"For one thing," said Sean. "We have coordinated backup and a plan. We've gotten in touch with your brother, and we're going to get them out."

"You're lying!" she screamed without thinking.

"I'm not lying, Emily," he said softly. "He knew you'd think I was. He said to tell you there's still a country mile for you to walk over again. I have no idea what the hell that's supposed to mean, but he said you'd understand."

Emily's eyes widened. *What if Sean is telling the truth? At the same time, what if he's lying? Can I trust him?* She chuckled nervously, "I can't stand down from this. I have to help him."

Sean and Candace stepped out of the glare, approaching slowly.

Sean said, "Sounded to me like he's got things under control. He said the Nomads are regrouping at the Arsenal with a large group of survivors. They need extraction. Some of them have been under fire. There are wounded civilians; we need to get moving to keep everyone safe."

Maybe I should trust them? "What about the monsters?"

He gestured at the burning horizon. "The reconnaissance squad that tipped us off to where you'd ended up has already encountered them. We know what we're up against, Emily. We're winning. I know you'd rather be involved. I get that. But it would be best for you to stand down and let us do our jobs."

Emily sniffed again, swallowing the lump in her throat. Her shoulders slumped and she rubbed at her eyes. Finally, she dropped the screwdriver, letting it clatter on the asphalt at her feet.

"So, this is how things end for me, huh? Everybody wants to keep me safe. No one wants me to fight. I know what I'm doing, too, dammit!"

Arms closed around her. "You've done enough fighting for now," Candace whispered. "None of you should ever have had to fight. "

19 Path to Reprieve

Valko brought up the rear as Joseph stalked at the front of their group. *He's distracted. What the hell did he and Maurice see in the comms building?* Steven was between them, every movement slow and methodical. The trip down the dormitory corridors and through the Nomad quarters had been thankfully uneventful.

A soft flutter passed through Valko's chest. The indignity of having hesitated when the fight with Blackwood went down weighed on his shoulders. Of course, it helped that Steven had found a way to not get Abaroa killed, by some miracle of movement. Even just looking at him, the fatigue was clear in his posture.

Steven looked like he could fall over any moment. On the thin line between courage, stupidity, and dumb luck, this poor bastard decided to tap dance. He was still looking for answers. Nothing was enough.

"Hey, Steven," Valko whispered. Steven turned to acknowledge the statement. "You've made her safe. That's what you wanted. Why are you still fighting?"

Steven slumped. "Because she's not safe. There's still more to do here. I have to see this through."

Valko said, "When this is over, what do we do?"

Steven smiled, stretching his shoulders and loosening his posture. "I try not to plan too far ahead. Too many people like to throw around words like 'premeditated'."

Joseph glanced back and snapped. "Stay focused. No telling what Richards has in store for us."

They reached the door at the end of the hallway. A plain-looking steel door with a card-scanner attached to the jamb.

The door slid open without a sound as they scanned Blackwood's ID. The three of them moved swiftly into the darkened room.

The lights snapped on, bright and clear. Desks and tables lined the room in semi-circles, various glass-walled laboratory rooms surrounding it. Corpses lay in disarray about the place.

A woman stood in the center of the large, round chamber. *Akuma-type.* She held a small body by its neck with a clawed hand. The small form was shaped like a Talon-type, and was covered in blood. She stared at the trio, eyes empty of emotion. Her hair was tangled and slick and dripping crimson. Valko and Steven held their pistols ready, as Joseph stood implacably, his rifle just a split-second motion from being fired.

Why do I feel ambushed? A single Akuma is a problem, for sure, but this feels wrong.

"Ah, boys," a voice called.

A light appeared in a room just behind her, set high into the wall. A slender man with a distinguished face, full gray hair, and immaculate spectacles glared down at them from behind thick glass, flanked by two black-uniformed figures with rifles. In his hand was a small frame, which he peered at longingly for a moment.

He set the frame down somewhere behind himself, then extended his arms to them like a king addressing his subjects.

The man had an angry, dangerous laugh, eyes appearing to glitter with manic energy behind the spectacles. "If you only knew how many years it took to create this project. How many sacrifices I made, understanding the human genome. The psychology of warfare. I have given you children the keys to immortality."

"Come on down, Richards," shouted Joseph, a distinct snarl in his voice. He aimed his rifle at Richards.

"That would be *Dr.* Richards to you, boy," Richards snapped. He took a deep breath and then continued speaking in a milder tone. "Dr. Osric Richards. If you miraculously manage to survive my dear wife, who I've taken extra care with preparing, it will be a name you should remember for the rest of your lives. You are, after all, my eternal legacy."

Valko growled. "The only thing eternal are the bodies you leave behind. How do you live with yourself?"

Clasping his hands behind him, Richards said with a crazed grin, "Poor, pretentious, deluded child. I saved her life with the virus. Harper's actions are to blame for the virus activating so quickly today. He just couldn't understand my vision."

Steven glared at Richards, but kept his Glock pointed at the woman. "Somehow, I doubt your wife wanted you to turn her into a monster."

Richards nodded. "As do I, my boy. She was to be the first Leviathan. My crowning achievement. Strength, speed, healing. Perfectly trained skills at the press of a button. A few more weeks of incubation, and she would have been ready for the next step. But now, she has all the power with no autonomy. The unchecked activation of the virus broke her mind."

The woman in the center of the room growled menacingly, dropping the small, broken body. Despite the fury, there was pain in her eyes. Tears streaked through the blood on her face. She stretched, audible pops issuing from her joints, filtering into the room to settle on the uncertain air.

Steven scowled. "You ever think about not sounding like a misogynistic ass? She ain't a trophy, and I get a feeling those tears aren't because she enjoys being like this."

"No, Steven," said Richards, sneering down at them, voice dripping with hatred. "And they aren't for you, either I'm afraid. As I said, the virus has broken her. That body beside her was our youngest child, Gram. Renee and Molly would have made wonderful additions to your group, but that didn't quite work out. They're all gone now."

The words hung in the air like dust, clinging to them, weighing them down. Valko's lungs filled and emptied numbly as he glanced between Richards's smug superiority, and the woman's barely bridled animal glare.

Richards glanced at his wristwatch and turned away with his guards. "Oh, would you look at the time? Boys, I wish you the best. Lanette, you are free to kill them as you see fit."

At the command, the woman sprang to the side, hurling a desk like it weighed nothing. The three ducked and scrambled into the chamber as the desk sailed over and smashed into a jumble of twisted metal scraps behind them.

Joseph fired a burst from his rifle, but Lanette slipped away from the bullets' path with ease, ducking low and rushing toward him. Valko intercepted her movement with a shot that went just a bit too far ahead of her.

Lanette snarled, sliding beneath another desk. She flipped it at Valko, and it struck him head-on. Cracks in his armor webbed out from the impact, and Valko skidded to a stop, pinned to another desk. Rage boiled within as the day's bizarre events settled into an undignified collage of death and destruction; all with Osric Richard's smiling face above it all.

Steven moved behind her, firing his Glock several times. A shot hit her in the shoulder, eliciting a scream. His aim was off. He was still reeling from his earlier injuries, it appeared. Lanette must have sensed it as well.

She swung a stool around, launching it at Steven. As it struck him, she was already rushing ahead at Joseph. Joseph methodically tracked her with his rifle, firing, but she weaved around the shots with inhuman speed.

Valko placed a boot against the desk and shoved with all his strength, sending it flying at her. She swatted it away and bounded over another. As she leaped, her clawed hand lashed out and Joseph's rifle fell from his hands in several ragged pieces.

Steven and Valko rushed in as Joseph dropped into a fighting stance. She swung the claw. Joseph parried the blow, landing a heavy punch to her armpit. She howled and drove an elbow down, cracking the shoulder plate of his armor.

Steven stumbled, body failing. He looked on in horror, legs crumpling beneath him. He fired off another shot that punched into the back of Lanette's thigh, then he collapsed.

Joseph buckled under the weight of the blow and turned, kicking out at a knee. She lifted her leg away from the blow and dropped it, pinning his legs.

Lanette shoved her claws down, deep into Joseph's chest. A gurgling scream erupted from him.

Valko smashed into her with everything he had, cracked armor shattering in places. They rolled across the floor until he straddled her. He slammed the butt of the shotgun into her face, then flipped it around and shoved the barrel into her mouth.

She grabbed the shotgun by the barrel as it fired. A portion of her face and hand burst. She screamed and shoved him with her good hand, ripping the shotgun from his hand as he flew back.

Valko landed on his back, broken armor starting to weigh him down more than it helped. To his left, Joseph was bleeding on the floor. To his right, Steven fought against reality itself, his body not responding to his desperate pleas for more strength.

Lanette stood slowly, her now misshapen face grimacing at the lot of them. Portions of flesh seemed to melt into one another, the muscles reknitting.

Her voice was quiet, husky, and slurred from a mouth full of blood, she said, "Poor, little pawns." A trail of blood droplets followed her. "To become involved with my husband is to embrace death. Were you the test of my skills, or was I the test of yours?"

"The hell," wheezed Valko as he reached up. He unsnapped and removed his helmet. He dropped it beside him and started working at the straps that held the Ferro-ceramic plates in place.

"Like I care." Joseph sat up with a grunt and hurled a grenade.

Lanette smacked the grenade back. It exploded in Joseph's face. His helmet and chest plate shattered and the force from the blast slammed him into the wall behind.

Joseph coughed up blood. Grimacing, he slumped against the wall with a curse.

"Is this the best my husband could create?" Lanette tilted her head, matted brown hair hanging limply. "So, what will you do, Nomads?"

Well, shit. What will we do? We're getting our asses handed to us.

A gun reported and her leg buckled as the shot hit. Another hit her arm. Joseph and Steven were both firing pistols, their shots hitting their marks. Lanette howled and doubled over. She had slowed enough. Valko grabbed one of the knives from its sheath on his discarded chest plate and darted in as the firing stopped.

He whirled the knife in a flash of silver, slashing into her flesh. As she staggered back, he flipped the blade around and slammed it into her chest. The blade scraped as it crackled through the sternum. He brought his free hand up, smashing his fist into her gut.

Ignoring the blood spilling on him, Valko heaved up Lanette and slammed her onto the dense metal lab desk. The seven-inch blade snapped, leaving just the hilt in his hand. A portion of the metal protruded from the center of her caved-in chest.

Valko hefted his shotgun from where it had fallen, hesitating as he saw the look on her face. A strange, peaceful glow had replaced the sadness and rage. The eyes, which had appeared red before, faded to a soft, deep brown of garden loam.

Tears streamed out of Lanette's eyes, cutting paths in the dried blood on her face. The skin beneath paled, and her eyelids fluttered without rhythm. With every breath, blood oozed around the embedded knife blade.

"I…feel like me again. Oh, God, it hurts so much."

Valko's face grew hot, seeing her in such weakness. She squirmed, but only her torso moved. The knife blade held her firmly in place.

"You have to stop him," she whimpered. "Stop Osric. Our daughters. Our son. Everything is ruined. Gone, because of him."

Valko trembled, swallowing thickly past a lump in his throat. The pressure behind his breastbone built like boiling water. *Why is my nose running?* Lanette gazed at him piteously. She breathed in, the sound of metal scraping against bone audible in the silence.

"Please," she whispered, staring into his eyes, "I'm so tired of living as a monster."

At once, Valko understood. This monster had been a person. She had been someone's child. Someone's wife. Someone's mother. All of it was taken from her. Rubbing an arm across his warm, wet face, Valko placed the barrel of the shotgun against her temple. Like a deadly kiss good night.

Valko spoke softly. "I'm so sorry you've had to suffer like this. I promise you; we'll stop him."

Behind him, Joseph groaned. "Service in honor..."

Brittle and hoarse, Steven croaked. "Hope in brotherhood..."

Valko blinked through the tears, looking her in the eyes. "Victory in sacrifice..."

He squeezed the trigger, the shotgun's blast seeming to echo longer than any other, settling in with finality. He dropped the weapon and moved to help Steven stay on his feet. They trudged to the wall where Joseph lay, the blood pooling around him.

Joseph choked, "Dammit, Valko. What the hell, man?" His chest heaved with pained sobs.

Valko's heart plummeted. Joseph had never cried in the ten years Valko had known him. He was the team's emotional center. Always cool and calm. That dangerous edge to the way he looked at everyone. This was the young man crying in front of Valko and Steven.

"I'm glad you guys are going to get him," he said. "This is some bullshit."

Steven grabbed Joseph's hand. "Come on, Cross. Let's get you to Nyura."

Joseph turned to look at him, but his eyes went too far to the side. As though sightless. "As much as I'd love to, I'm not making it that far. I'm sorry, Steven. You can't save everyone."

He turned back, coughing more blood. "Valko. Steven. Find Emily for me. Tell her I'm sorry. Tell her I love her."

"Yes, sir," Valko whispered, gripping his friend's other hand. "Fade into silence, brother."

Joseph fell still with a final shudder.

Valko slumped in front of Joseph's body, wracked with sudden trembling. A particularly painful silence settled in the room. *Damn. What do we do now?*

"What we always do," Steven said weakly. "Get up and keep fighting. That's all there is. That's all there *ever* is."

Valko hadn't realized he'd spoken his thoughts aloud. He turned to stare helplessly at Steven's tear-streaked face. One of Steven's eyes had swollen shut, and his face was darkening with deep bruises. Steven's good eye fluttered, his breathing fast and shallow; lips pressed to a tight line. Despite all that, Steven looked emptied of emotion, like a stone in a stream.

The door finally burst open; the twisted remnants of the desk shoved out of the way. Nikifor led a squad of ten soldiers who swept into the room, surveying the chaos with wide-eyed stares.

Nikifor moved in and embraced Valko and Steven. "It's over," he said.

For his part, however, Valko felt no relief. Fury buried all other emotion. He swallowed to keep from screaming as he took in the corpses around him. There couldn't be solace for the day's events until they found and stopped Dr. Osric Richards.

He would pay for his hubris. For playing God in all the lives he'd touched. And Valko would be there to see him fall. He had to, now that he'd made such a promise.

20 Life After The War

The tightness in Steven's chest was akin to a closed fist squeezing his heart. He stared off into the tree line from the open cabin window. A bead of sweat formed on his face from the unseasonably warm mountain weather.

How the hell did we go an entire state away from Blue Rock and end up on another damn mountain?

Despite the attempt to diffuse his thoughts with humor, a strange sound escaped him. He closed his eyes, trying to let the Chaplain's well-rehearsed words of comfort help him like they did before. But there were too many dead. Too many graves.

Steven whispered to himself, "The sufferings of this present time..."

He had to admit, healing at a faster than normal rate could have its perks. Only weeks after the fighting, and he just had the occasional stitch in his side if he pushed himself too hard. Covered in only scars now, Steven had recovered enough to do his usual maintenance drills. Although, with remarkably less enthusiasm than before.

Steven turned from the pleasant scene of the tree line, forcing himself numb to the faces of the lost. Valko and Nikifor were sitting on one of the beds, talking quietly. He appreciated their presence. And, if nothing else, the distinct lack of Antoine's. He hadn't told anyone where he would go while they awaited whatever the newly appointed oversight committee fated for them, and no one seemed to care.

In a way, he suspected the Stoyan brothers felt the same. The two stopped talking and looked up at him when they noticed his attention.

Valko tilted his chin in question. "You good?"

Steven shrugged. "Not really."

"Yeah," sighed Valko. "Me neither."

Steven blew out a slow breath, sitting on the bed across from them.

"Look at the bright side," said Nikifor, a soft smile on his lips. "Grace's dad seems to have taken a shine to you."

Steven said, "You can't be serious. He scowls at me every time he hears me breathing too heavily."

Nikifor raised a hand. "But he never pointed the shotgun at you."

Snorting, Steven shook his head. "True. I suppose not being threatened works."

His phone chimed and he snatched it from the side table. He pressed the button. He'd missed several text messages from Grace. She'd become a fixture in his life, but he wasn't quite used to it. She confused him, and he was certain he didn't know what he was doing. Steven wondered if he'd ever feel like he deserved her.

He set the phone back on the table, hunching over and rubbing his hands together methodically. He wasn't ready to face what she had to say; he suspected it would be another reminder of how he needed to be kind to himself.

Needing to shift his mind to something he understood, he gazed across the room at the brothers. "I don't understand how he got away. He couldn't have been that far ahead of the National Guard."

"It's simple, Steven." Nikifor sucked at his teeth, steepling his fingers. "We were behind the curve. We got played from the very beginning. And the National Guard had a lot on their hands just trying to catch up with everything we already had a handle on. Richards was prepared, simple as that."

Valko groaned. "Still doesn't explain why those CIA assholes wouldn't tell us anything. They've got to know something, right?"

Nikifor looked at him pointedly. "Yeah, like they're going to trust a bunch of hormonal teens holding guns with government secrets. Don't kid yourself, Val."

"How the hell am I supposed to tell Emily anything if I don't know where she is?" Valko shouted, punching the mattress. Thinking about Emily and how they'd tell her Joseph didn't make it made Steven's stomach tie in knots.

"Calm your ass down, Rambo." Nikifor leaned back. "Maybe they don't know where she is. Considering the kill-squads sent after us, she probably got herself hidden somewhere safe. Give it time, and maybe she'll call us."

"Right," snapped Valko. "You telling me you trust these-"

"No," said Nikifor, coldly. "There's nothing we can do about it, so stop stressing so damn hard. We'll figure it all out, and we'll find her. I'm telling you to trust *me*."

Valko deflated into himself, the anger fading. Only Nikifor could cause that reaction. *There's just something about that coldness. It's strange to think anger can be cold.*

There was a knock at the door. The three of them glanced in that direction, but no one moved. A second knock and Nikifor stood with a sigh, opening the door.

Grace and Mirena entered, wearing matching t-shirts and shorts, towels across their shoulders.

Mirena stalked straight to Steven, arms crossed, and eyebrows knit, like a parent scolding a child. She hissed at him, "Is there a reason you're ignoring your phone, Esteban?"

Steven leaned over to look past Mirena, watching Grace enter the room with more trepidation, shoulders hunched. The dark, disappointed look in her eye made him ashamed of himself.

Steven dropped his gaze to the floor. "Can you really blame me? You've hated me since I saved you at school. Every time I close my eyes, I see blood and smoke. Every time I open them, I have to answer questions like this. All I'm saying is, nobody bothered me this much when I was dead."

"Look, I'm sorry, okay?" Mirena wrapped her arms around him. "How many times do I have to apologize for being scared out of my mind? You try figuring out one of your best friends—and for that matter, the guy your cousin is interested in dating–is a gun-toting maniac while your teacher tries to kill you without using boredom."

Valko snorted, and everyone stared at him. He shrugged. "What? It was funny."

Steven was startled to see Mirena absentmindedly licking her lips, staring transfixed at Valko's bare chest. Steven, at once, was aware of his lack of a shirt, and that of his friends. They had not been expecting the girls to show up in their room. She let go of Steven and intentionally flopped down on the bed next to Valko, pushing her hair behind an ear.

Mirena made herself comfortable, leaning back on her hands. "A man with a sense of humor. Adios, Esteban! Hola, nene bonito."

Valko raised an eyebrow. "Did you just call me a fish?"

Biting her lip, Mirena said, "Only if you kiss like one. Otherwise, I called you a pretty boy."

Nikifor shook his head, grinning, and picked up his shirt. "On that note, I'm going to make myself scarce and spend some of this stipend money on something pointless."

Grace nodded, a half-smile forming on her lips. 'That's...actually the reason we came over here. We wanted to invite you guys to the pool for a swim, then dinner."

Nikifor stopped to lean against the room's provided chest of drawers with an eyebrow raised. The smile on his face hinted at what could only be amusement.

Steven smiled at her. "So, graduated from asking a guy to the dance, all the way to asking a guy to dinner? Somebody's gotten bold."

Why do I feel like he set me up?

Grace's face broke into a genuine, soft smile. "Maybe, and...?"

"Sounds good to me," he said, dragging his shirt from the other side of the bed. "Let's get moving before Mirena confuses Valko with all the flirting. He's young and impressionable."

"Culo!" Mirena's towel slapped Steven in the face as the five of them laughed together. He tried to ignore the flare of pain behind his left eye.

Grace put her hands up. "To be fair, you are kind of throwing yourself at him."

Mirena put her hands on her hips. "Oh, I was? You don't gotta worry 'bout me, nena. Not my fault if young and impressionable means the man in the room knows what he likes."

Grace's face went red. "Some days, I wonder why I spend so much time with you."

"But why, nena?" Mirena put a finger to her lips and batted her eyes at Grace. "I'm such a lovely cousin. I'm taking one for the team, love. Just one more handsome piece of competition away from your man, and all that. Isn't that right, Val?"

Valko rubbed at the back of his neck and blew a soft breath. He looked like a feral cat, all hackles and prepared to bolt away at top speed.

Steven said, "Sorry. You get used to the attention."

Valko shrugged, but his posture didn't relax.

"Who knows," said Mirena. "Maybe they both like the curves, but Steven's too much of a gentleman to say so."

Grace poked her tongue out. "Yeah, I'm sure boys like it when you're poured into your clothes but forgot to say when."

Steven and Valko both winced, but Mirena laughed so hard, her eyes shone with tears. She got up and threw her arms around Grace.

"Nena," she singsonged. "You can't act like a Chola anywhere but in front of your man, and it's so adorable."

Grace pushed her away with a giggle. Mirena plopped back down next to Valko.

"Sorry, nene," she said to him. "Where were we?"

Nikifor's phone chimed, and he looked at it. He answered it, shaking his head on his way out the door. "Hey, Ladeen. What's up?"

Mirena raised an eyebrow. "Oh? That was the girl who worked in the office during her free period, yeah?"

Steven said, "Yeah. She's still torn up about Curtis."

Mirena nodded solemnly. "I'm glad she's got someone she can call for help with those feelings." She pointed a glare at Steven, her voice almost a growl. "It helps to let people know you're okay."

"But I'm not okay. Not sure I ever was." He shrugged, eyes falling again to the floor.

"Hey." A hand on his shoulder brought him back. He looked up into Grace's kind eyes. They reminded him of a forest glade;

beautiful and serene. "None of us are going to be over any of that. Not any time soon. The people we lost would want us to keep going. So, that's what we'll do. Keep moving forward, and not giving up."

More than anything else, Steven ached to pull her into an embrace. He hesitated. *Are we ready for that? I've spent far too much time in a fog these past few weeks. I don't know what I'm doing.*

She tugged at his shoulder, and he stood. She wrapped him in a tight hug. He returned it, heart hammering. She pulled away and looked into his face.

"You know what?" she said, "Forget the pool. It's cold out anyway, and I'm starving. What do you want to eat?"

Mirena chimed in, "Don't fall for the trap, Esteban. She's baiting you into your first argument!"

Steven laughed. "Sounds like you've got a suggestion?"

"Hell yeah!" she said, "Checked out the local guide. Gafas del Sol is playing live at that place down the way. We passed it on our way in. All we gotta do is grab a table between three and six?"

Valko looked at the clock on the bedside table with a brow raised.

"You do realize it's one-thirty right now."

"Your point?"

"I don't know about Steven, but I'm wearing almost everything I own right now."

Steven looked down. "I think I've got two white t-shirts and literally this pair of pants."

Mirena's mouth dropped open, and she stared between them. "Are you freaking serious right now? Bro, we're down here with two vehicles and as many stores as we've all gone to, with and without Uncle Robert, and neither one of you so much as bought a pair of pants? Do you walk to the laundry room naked? Do you even wash your clothes? Do you wash yourselves? You've got money now, what else you gonna spend it on? Con que tipo de bárbaros viajo? Chicos apestosos, malditos!"

Grace stopped her with a hand wave. She showed Mirena her phone. "Miri, honey. Take a breath. We have time. We have my car. There's a store only twenty minutes from here. Now, can we please stop talking about naked boys in front of naked boys?"

With her last couple of words, Grace winked at Steven, and he put his face in his hands, groaning.

Oh, lord. Of all the things to prepare me for, Dad. Why didn't you say anything about this? How do I even respond here?

When the girls left the room to get ready, Steven padded to the bathroom and picked up his shirt, slipping it on. They'd had to leave a lot behind in Blue Rock, on account of whatever wasn't on fire was likely covered in blood.

Steven wondered, not for the first time, if some group was going to analyze the data they gathered and come after him for study. He imagined a bunch of guys hopping out of a van to take him into forced custody, testing his blood for traces of the nano-virus, and-

He stared at his reflection in the mirror. A significant portion of his face was still yellow-brown from the bruising. He was lucky the orbital fracture hadn't taken his left eye completely. He pressed fingers into a bruise, the sharp pain a gentle reminder.

Valko clapped him on the shoulder on his way to the shower. "Yeah, Sage. You still look like hell."

Steven gripped the counter. His eyes narrowed, the shooting pain on the left side still pronounced. He'd finally managed to stop wincing every time his eyes adjusted in their sockets, but damn if it didn't sting.

"Sorry," said Valko. "I like it. It fits you. And, considering you've got more experience on the civilian side, you're kind of the de facto leader in this situation. Cross always insisted on his code name, regardless."

Steven forced a smile. "Kind of helps that his call sign just so happened to also be his last name, though."

Valko laughed. "There, now you got it. Smiling like that probably hurts like hell right now, don't it?"

"Yeah."

Two hours of shopping, and everyone had new clothes. The time had flown by, but Steven could have gone the rest of his life without having to parade around in front of Mirena and Valko wearing various combinations of shirts and pants. Apparently, Mirena was a fashion guru as well as a love guru--at least in her own words.

Steven shook off the annoyance from the forced shopping trip as they walked up to the restaurant's entrance. He had never seen one with two stories before. It was a huge building and built at a fork in the highway. He caught himself clocking the corners and balconies, squinting at the dark places as they followed the hostess.

Grace laced her arm with his and gave it a light squeeze. The band finished their setup as Grace excitedly pulled him toward a stairwell in the back. A neon sign hung on the wall behind the bar.

Love brought me in here. Love will see me out.

Steven let her lead him up the stairs. A guy on his way down let his eyes wander a bit, lingering on Grace, before they landed on Steven's new shirt.

"Oh, dude!" said the guy, pointing. "Awesome Charizard shirt!"

Steven looked at his own shirt, with its dragon silhouetted in flames boldly claiming his chest with a roar.

He said, "That's what it's called? Thanks! These knuckleheads wouldn't tell me."

The guy looked at him funny. He apparently noticed the bruising, because he cautiously glanced at Grace again. His eyes went just a little too wide.

I just can't go anywhere without being scary, huh?

Recovering, the guy said, "You don't know...about Pokémon?"

Steven did his best to smile. "I don't get out much. All I know is it's angry, and it's on fire. It's practically family."

The guy laughed nervously and hurried down the stairs, passing Valko and Mirena, disappearing around the corner without a backward glance.

As they reached the landing, the hostess guided them to a table next to the balcony with a great view of the wide stage. The band was starting to play. They had an infectious energy, the trumpets bleating in time with guitar riffs and percussive snaps. Steven could see why this would be Mirena's favorite band. *Just some pretty little planned chaos.*

Grace leaned into his ear and whispered, "I bet he thinks I beat you."

Her breath tickled his neck and he grinned. "Good for him. After checking you out like that, I half expected you to clock him."

"I couldn't do that," Grace half-whined, eyes softening. She was chewing on her lip as she gazed into his eyes.

"Well, that's good." Steven leaned in. "Because you don't scare me."

"Oh, yeah, tough guy?" Grace's voice grew breathy. It was taking her longer and longer to exhale with every intake. "Then why's your heart beating so fast?"

"Because you're too beautiful for me." He found himself whispering. "I'm warning you, now."

Grace's breath halted a moment as a hand fluttered to her chest. "Warning me about what?"

Licking his lips, Steven said, "If you keep looking at me like you want me to kiss you, I just might do it."

Steven leaned in, brushing his stinging lips against Grace's. The pain settled to a dull roar, as pleasure overtook it. His breath caught when she pressed back into the kiss.

21 Epilogue

Emily sat in a metal folding chair on the supermarket roof, a bright green apron draped on the back of it. The novel in her hands, although newer than the last few, was already starting to fray at the edges. She needed to invest in a bag of some sort. Her pockets always did a number on these poor, bound worlds of fantasy.

A brunette sat smoking a joint nearby, smiling her way. The girl's legs dangled from the air conditioner unit. She was maybe a few years older, mid-twenties at the oldest.

Crystal said, "C'mon, chick. Just try some already. It's good for you."

"Can you even hear me?" Emily replied, shaking her head. "I'll only say it one more time. No, thank you."

"Emmie, girl, would it kill you to loosen up?"

Emily blew out a breath. "Maybe not this time. But, eventually, yes. I keep myself safe by being ready, and not altering my mental state with that garbage. You do what you want to, but just know you'd be really easy to mug right now."

"You're mad crazy, Emmie." The other girl laughed. It was a soft, tinkling sound. A reminiscence of her name. She put the joint back to her lips and puffed.

Emily placed a bookmark. "Only if it's crazy to be prepared."

Crystal sneered with a playful wink. "That what the knife is for? You gonna mug me? Just make sure it's rough enough, doll."

Emily rolled her eyes. "Ample though you are, dear, I'm simply not interested."

"Ooh, that's such a sneaky and pretty way to call me fat. I'll need to remember that." Crystal inhaled deep and spat out phlegm on the rooftop to her other side. "No guys, no girls. You're not interested in much, are you?"

Emily sat back in her chair. She'd had this conversation before. It never ended well.

"What's the point?" asked Emily with a shrug.

Crystal's eyes went wide like saucers for a bit, then narrowed as she grinned and hopped off the air conditioner unit. She ambled over toward the edge of the roof. She howled into the night and lifted her shirt, shaking her figure in the frigid night air.

Putting her shirt down, Crystal turned back with fists on her hips. "To loosen up and enjoy yourself! That's the point, Emmie. Some days, all we do is make it. We survive. But some days, doll, you gotta really live."

Emily rolled her eyes again. She couldn't fathom the level of thoughtlessness there was to this young woman's worldview. Whether or not there could be any point to the conversation was left to be seen. Crystal sauntered back toward her former perch.

Sighing, Emily said, "How much of that did you smoke? Life sucks, so live fast and die young, right? How the hell is that better?" Putting a hand up, she took in a calming breath. "I've lost enough friends. Throwing away my own safety for a night of what you call 'fun' is in the bad things category for me. I just can't get behind that."

Crystal twisted her hips, dancing without music. She closed her eyes and whirled, a smile on her lips underneath the false stars of the city lights around her. She stopped spinning and gyrating and looked at Emily. Like, really looked. Her eyes were rimmed in red.

"Newsflash, baby doll," said Crystal, stretching her arms out wide. "That's growing up. You're not the only little girl to lose someone close to you when you were younger."

Of course, Crystal was right about that. Emily's heart sank a little, considering what this young woman must have endured. The haughtiness, however. She narrowed her eyes and glared at Crystal.

"Not long ago, I left my brother," she growled, "to be gutted by a monster."

Emily wanted to scream the words as the bile rose in her throat, and the rage beneath her surface threatened to take physical form.

"Your brother? Damn. You're so strong." Crystal stopped moving. Her eyes were glued to Emily's face.

Frowning, Emily pulled the folding knife from her pocket and opened it. "Screw being strong. Strength is meaningless at the wrong end of the right weapon."

Crystal tilted her head. "I don't get it."

The words spilled unbidden. "If I had pushed just a bit further. If I had moved just a bit faster. I killed another girl my age with a number two Phillips-head screwdriver, just trying to come to his rescue. Someone convinced me I'd fought enough, and I listened. He's dead now because I didn't go far enough."

Crystal stood, mouth agape.

Staring, Emily noted Crystal's trembling. "I know the difference between fiction and reality. I know people die. Every moment of every day. But, until you're actually responsible for the deaths around you, you don't have the credentials to belittle my experience."

"I didn't-"

"I don't judge you for how you choose to escape this reality." Emily waggled her novel at Crystal. "This is my escape. This is my drug. Those chemicals you smoke, sex, the human body? None of those hold any mysteries for me. I've experienced all I intend to of what can be done to a person."

"But-" She still looked confused. Like her brain needed time to catch up to the words.

Emily stood, retrieving her apron. "Don't worry about it. Come on. Pretty sure our break time is over."

Crystal grabbed her own lime green apron hanging from the air conditioner, pouting with trembling lips and eyes. For such a robust young woman, she resembled a scolded five-year-old at that moment.

Emily wondered at the numb feeling in her own chest. She didn't exactly feel bad about her outburst, but it probably wasn't warranted either. She glanced at her new phone on the way down the stairs. It had only been a few months since what was being termed the 'Blue Rock Incident'.

Since Joseph died. They never let me see his body. His grave. Never let me say goodbye. Maybe that's why. How can I have a decent Friday, when every Friday is nothing more than a reminder?

The two of them entered the backrooms of the supermarket in silence. Emily excused herself to the restroom, where she washed her hands and face, glaring into her own eyes. Some of her freckles had darkened and her nose was still a bit off-center. Her hair still reminded her of Joseph. Too many things reminded her of Joseph.

Emily walked out of the restroom and moved to the stock area, grabbing a cart stacked with produce. Trudging out to the sales floor with the cart in tow, she ignored Crystal chatting up a young man stocking a shelf of crackers.

Moving to the carrot display, Emily sorted and stacked the vegetables in silence, her motions rote, her mind wandering. Someone tapped her shoulder.

Turning, Emily found herself face to face with a man in his late thirties, maybe early forties. The man wore some ugly designer polo shirt and jeans. The watch on his wrist barely fit him, glittering under the fluorescent bulbs.

"How can I help you?" she said, pasting a smile on.

The man beamed, although the smile didn't quite reach his eyes. "My, my, aren't you a pretty one? And such a radiant smile."

Emily crossed her arms over her chest, meeting the man's blank gaze. There was a look in his eyes. Something feral, primal.

He shook his head and chuckled. "I'm sorry, that was rude of me. Could you direct me to the kombucha? I think they've moved it from its usual spot."

Emily nodded. "Sure, right this way."

She turned on her heel and led him around the aisles to a refrigerated drinks section.

"Is this it?" He frowned at the display of glass-bottled health drinks, chewing on his bottom lip and looking lost.

"Is there a particular flavor you're looking for? Maybe I can check in the back?"

"No," he said, turning to leer at her, his gaze like a flame as he raked it up and down her body. "I don't think I'll find what I'm looking for here. Unless, of course, I got your phone number."

Emily squinted at him. "I'm not having a great day. And I'm definitely not what you're looking for."

He stepped in and put out a hand, touching her cheek. "Don't be like that."

Grabbing the hand, Emily twisted a finger until it bent awkwardly, and the man grunted in pain.

He cursed loudly, drawing attention from nearby.

She whispered, "You want your fingers bagged in paper or plastic? Touch me again, and your head goes through the glass behind you."

"Where is your manager!" he screamed. His face was the color of liver. "Do you have any idea who I am?"

"Gonna get me fired?" She grinned. "Play with fire if you want to."

Crystal, the young stocker she was flirting with, and the manager on duty all came around the corner at a fast walk. The man in front of her was practically foaming as he screamed.

"Sir?" The manager put his hands up with palms out. "What's going on here?"

"I asked where the kombucha was, and this dumb bitch broke my finger."

Emily smiled sweetly as the manager took in the scene, processing the words. He narrowed his eyes at her, then shifted them back to the man.

"Oh," she said, "such a big, strong man? You must usually get away with inappropriately and non-consensually touching minors. Should I have let your hands wander? You deserve far worse than me shoving your greasy fingers off my body."

The manager pinched the bridge of his nose. "Sir, is that true? Did you touch her?"

The man shifted. "I was-"

"Before you lie," said Emily, "look up and to your left at the mounted camera, jackass. Make sure you smile."

The manager sighed. "Sir, I'm going to have to ask you to leave the premises before I call the police."

His eyes darted between her and the manager, eyebrows knit. "Why? Because my hand accidentally brushed her face?"

Shaking her head, Emily crossed her arms. "While you were reaching for the cooler behind you? Try again. Or admit to yourself you made a mistake and got creepy with the wrong redhead. Walk away. Or don't. Totally your choice."

The man's eyes narrowed, and he glared daggers at her.

She shook her head. "Listen, hot shot. I have a job to do. I'm going to get back to it while you decide how to move on with your pathetic, lecherous life. May your five-year-old neighbor have their violin practice during all of your hangovers."

Emily turned to walk away, and a hand grabbed her roughly by the elbow. She looked sidelong at the man's hand, shifting her amused glare up to his sneering face.

"No," the man hissed. "You're going to jail for assault."

She smiled. "Maybe."

The way the man's eyes changed as the word sunk in and he took a second look sparked joy within her heart. Whipping her arm around, she broke his grip with ease, striking him in the throat with her other hand. He spluttered a moment before she grabbed him by the face and smashed his head into the glass door. Being safety glass, it shattered into millions of small shards that cascaded to the floor. He slumped down, bleeding and choking, eyes wide.

Emily wiped her elbow with her apron, face scrunched in disgust. "Touch me a third time for the grand prize. A free trip to the mortuary."

"Emma," the manager said firmly as he pulled a phone from his pocket. A crowd had begun gathering. "Step away from that man and go to the office, please. Go sit and calm down. This doesn't need to continue."

Calm down? This is calm.

If only she weren't so annoyed, Emily would have smiled as someone nearby cheered.

Emily looked back at the manager. "It didn't need to start. If he didn't touch me, I wouldn't have defended myself. Simple as that. And get my damn name right."

"To the office, please, while we get this sorted out," the manager insisted, looking haggard. He turned his attention back to the phone and the scene before him. "Yes, I need to report an altercation. No one's in danger. It's over. Yes, I need police and EMS. No, no weapons involved."

Emily took her apron off, gently folding it in her arms. Tucking it under an arm, she walked away toward the back of the store. She sucked at her teeth.

Crystal's mouth hung open like a dead fish, eyes wide in shock. She took a step back as Emily passed by.

She must have thought I'd exaggerated everything. Trying to sound cool.

"Reality sucks, yeah?" Emily whispered as she passed by.

A half-hour later, Emily sat in an office chair, reciting the same information a third time to yet another cop. The manager had long since taken the information down into an incident report. He'd made a copy of the video surveillance feed for the officers and was packaging the disk.

A soft knock at the door was followed by a woman walking in, wearing a nice navy-colored suit. She was followed by a heavy-set man in an equally nice suit, though much rougher in appearance, like it had seen the wrong side of a chimney. Or maybe he just never had it cleaned. Who knew?

Agent Candace Haig presented her credentials to the officers and manager, gesturing back to Sean Brodus before closing the door behind her.

She set her bag on the desk. "To put things simply, I need those reports for redaction and summary destruction."

"Ma'am?" said the officer.

"Yes, Officer?"

"This young woman was involved in an assault. The man she assaulted is intent on pressing charges."

"Oh, her appointed lawyers are discussing that situation with his. He'll be withdrawing those charges."

"She put the man's head through a glass door."

"After repeated attempts at sexual assault of a minor, attempted grooming of a minor, verbal assault, intentional harassment, and tampering with a witness of a major crime under investigation with relation to national security. Yes, his lawyer is being brought up to speed on how things will go, should he choose to pursue this matter. Meanwhile, the reports have to go."

"Ma'am, I'm sorry," said the officer with a shrug. "You don't have the authority to order that."

Sean produced a folded paper from his pocket, handing it to Candace. She unfolded it and handed it to the officer. He stared between the paper and the two agents in front of him for a few long moments, lips pressed in a tight line.

After a while, Candace cleared her throat. "I do, actually. I'm not ordering anything yet, Sergeant. I am, however, strongly requesting. Operations Officer Brodus and I are working with a joint agency task force, assigned to a case of significant national security."

Candace paused a moment, then gestured at Emily. "This young woman is a key witness in an ongoing federal investigation. Should you deny my request further, it may become necessary for me to contact the person that will order the destruction of those documents, along with disciplinary actions regarding your impediment to my investigation. I'm trying to do this without stepping on your authority."

The cop rubbed at the back of his neck. "I still don't feel comfortable with this... I need to confer with my superiors. But, as far as I'm concerned, this girl is in a lot of trouble."

Candace cut her eyes at Emily. "She most certainly is."

Emily rolled her eyes. "Seriously?"

"Emily," Sean said softly.

"Don't you dare say my name like you care," Emily snapped. She took a deep breath and sighed. "I hate that I listened to you once. You talked me out of saving my brother. You've kept me isolated from my friends, who could help to keep me safe. I'm stuck in this overrated tourist trap away from anyone that actually cares about me. How, exactly, are you any better than Blackwood again?"

Sean's eyes narrowed. "We're not torturing you, for one thing."

"You haven't fed me yet," Emily said, sourly. "That counts as torture."

Candace cleared her throat. "Listen, Emily. Until we know how that girl tracked you down, you're under our protection. That, unfortunately, means isolation from anyone who might not have cut ties."

Raising an eyebrow, Emily glanced between the adults. "Protection? It took you thirty minutes to get here. Life and death are determined in seconds, not minutes, and you know it. Anyone they might send after me is going to be at least as good as that girl, if not better. You can't sell dreams to a girl who lives in her nightmares."

Emily ignored the wide-eyed looks on the cop's faces, but she did catch the nod of agreement from the sergeant.

Sean sighed. "We've been trying to stay out of your way as much as we can while we figure all this out. In exchange, you keep a low profile. That was the deal, Emily. Allow me to reiterate that we are not inclined to negotiate terms with you."

Emily gripped the sides of her head and blew out a heavy breath. Her face warmed. Everything welled up from within. Rage, shame, and inaction choked her.

"You told me to trust you!" Emily spilled the words, louder than intended. She quieted her voice. "That I shouldn't have to fight."

Candace shook her head, but Sean blustered. "You interfered with the plan. Delayed my timeline. What do you want from me, kid?"

Palms pressed against her eyes, Emily sobbed, "I want my brother back."